"You never liked me, Dakota."

She frowned at that, cast him a sidelong look, then turned her attention to the rolling countryside.

"I didn't hate you."

"Didn't say *hate*," he said. "But you didn't much like me, either."

She shrugged in acceptance of that, and he smiled at the irony. He'd never bonded with a woman before over her general dislike of him.

"The thing is, you never fell for my act."

"So you admit it was an act," she shot back.

"Sure." He shrugged. "Every guy has an act." What man wanted to advertise the things that hurt?

"Is this an act now?"

"I've got nothing left to fake," he said quietly. "I'm the least popular guy in town trying to hold things together for my brother. Don't worry. I know where I stand with you."

Color rose in her cheeks, and she looked away again. "I should get to bed, Andy."

"You should." He'd known she wouldn't stay out with him long, but it had been nice, all the same. There was something about being alone with Dakota under the big Montana sky that woke up a part of him that had been dormant for too long...

Dear Reader,

Even the best of us mess up, and it makes it worse when there is a solid reputation at stake. When I wrote Chet's story in *Her Stubborn Cowboy*, I realized that I really liked Andy. He was a man who had made mistakes, but he wasn't a bad man. In fact, he deserved a second chance to find his place in Hope, Montana. And who better to throw into his path than the woman who hates him most?

Christmastime is about redemption. Every family has that black sheep, the one who took the path less traveled, the one who shocked everyone with some life choice or other. If you're that black sheep, then you know how hard it is to go home again. It isn't just the criticism; it's the simple fact that you've changed, and you can't help that. The biggest risk we ever take is to return home and say "Is there a place for me...still?"

I hope you have a home to return to at holiday time. I hope you have people who love you and forgive you for being human. Because we're all human, and sometimes the most "perfect" family members who arrive at family gatherings with cherubic children and Jell-O salad are the closest to snapping and losing it. So take some solace in that!

May this Christmas bring you home—to the family that drives you crazy and that you love anyway. Merry Christmas from my home to yours!

Patricia Johns

THE COWBOY'S CHRISTMAS BRIDE

PATRICIA JOHNS

HARLEQUIN® WESTERN ROMANCE®

Recycling programs
for this product may
not exist in your area.

ISBN-13: 978-0-373-75735-0

The Cowboy's Christmas Bride

Copyright © 2016 by Patty Froese Ntihemuka

Printed in U.S.A.

Patricia Johns writes from northern Alberta, where she lives with her husband and son. The winters are long, cold and perfectly suited to novel writing. She has a BA in English lit, and you can find her books in Harlequin's Love Inspired and Harlequin Western Romance lines.

Books by Patricia Johns

American Romance

Hope, Montana

Safe in the Lawman's Arms
Her Stubborn Cowboy

Love Inspired

His Unexpected Family
The Rancher's City Girl
A Firefighter's Promise
The Lawman's Surprise Family

To my husband, the real-life guy who inspires my heroes: strong, stubborn and a heart that beats for me. Who could ask for more?

Chapter One

Andy Granger sat across from Dakota Mason—the one woman in Hope, Montana, who had never fallen for his charms. Yet here they were, and Dakota looked less than impressed to see him. A pile of ledgers teetered next to a mug of lukewarm coffee and outside a chill wind whistled, whipping crispy leaves across his line of sight through the side window. It was getting late in the winter for there to have not been snow yet, but it looked like it wouldn't hold off much longer.

Andy leaned his elbows on the table and pushed the coffee mug aside. "Didn't expect to see me here, did you?" he asked, a half smile toying at his lips.

Dakota pulled her fingers through her thick, chestnut hair, tugging it away from her face, cheeks still reddened from the cold outside. She'd always been beautiful; the years only seemed to improve her.

"I was expecting Chet," she said. "He said he needed some extra help on the cattle drive. I'd rather deal with him, if you don't mind."

Yeah, everyone was expecting Chet. Andy was

here for a couple of weeks at the most. He'd agreed to do the cattle drive this year for his brother and then he was heading back to his life in the city. This ranch—this town even—wasn't home anymore, and he'd been reminded of that little fact repeatedly since arriving.

"Afraid I can't oblige," he replied. "Chet and Mackenzie are in the city. There were some complications with her pregnancy. That can happen with twins, apparently. Anyway, I'm here to take care of things until they return."

That was why Chet had held off on their cattle run to bring the herd from the far pastures in the foothills back to the safety of nearby fields for the winter months. The warm fall and late winter had felt providential with Mack's problematic pregnancy, but the cattle had to come back soon, and now Andy would be the one to do it. As long as he was back out of town before Christmas, he'd call it a success.

"Mack's okay, though?" Dakota asked, her expression softening a little.

"Yeah, she'll be fine." He leaned back in his chair. "So, how've you been?"

"You haven't heard?" Dakota tugged her leather jacket a little closer around herself. She looked uncomfortable, not that Andy blamed her. Everyone seemed ill-at-ease around him since his return, and he'd rolled with it, but he didn't like seeing that discomfort in Dakota's eyes. She'd always been one of the few to see straight through his act—which had generally taken the form of telling him he was an idiot—and this time he wished she could still see what no one else seemed to…that he wasn't all bad.

"I've been out of the loop lately," he confessed.

"That's an understatement," she retorted. "But thanks to you selling off that land to developers, our ranch is now bone dry."

"What?" Andy frowned. "What are you talking about?"

"The streams that ran through your pasture watered ours," she said. "The developers blocked the main ones to make some sort of reservoir. We're down to a trickle."

"Sorry, I didn't know." Those words didn't encompass half of what he felt. That sale had been a mistake, and while he'd been able to buy a car dealership in the city, which had turned into a rather lucrative investment, he'd never been able to shake the certainty he'd made a monumental error when he sold his half of the inheritance and the family pasture.

"But glad to know you made some money off it." Her tone dripped sarcasm.

"It was my land to sell, Dakota."

It wasn't like he'd stolen something from his brother. What was he supposed to do—dutifully step back and forget about his inheritance altogether because his brother was using it?

"Yeah, but to Lordship Land Developers?" she snapped. He'd seen the sign beside the road, too—a bit of a jolt when he'd first driven back into town.

Dakota wasn't so far away from his position. Sure,

her parents were still alive, but every ranch faced the same problem. When the owner had more than one child, and the bulk of his financial worth was wrapped up in that land, how did you divide it in a will and still keep the business intact? Who got the ranch and who got cut out?

"What if your brother inherited your dad's ranch?" he pressed. "Let's say your dad leaves the whole thing to Brody. What if you were left with some scrub grass and some memories, and that was it? What if you were pushed out and had to find a way to deal? Are you telling me you wouldn't have done the same thing? It's not much of an inheritance when no one expects you to lay a finger on it."

"Then you sell to your brother," she said with a shake of her head. "But you didn't. You turned this grudge between you and Chet into something that put a black mark on this whole community. Who says anybody is okay with having some resort built here? We're a ranch community, not a vacation spot."

"Take it up with the mayor." He was tired of defending himself. Everyone had the same complaint—he'd sold to an outsider. That was the kind of misstep the town of Hope couldn't forgive.

"Trust me, we tried," she retorted. "Especially when our land dried up and we had to try and graze an entire herd on dust."

Andy's stomach sank. Was it that bad? It wasn't like he could've anticipated that, but people around here didn't seem to care about what was fair to blame on him and what wasn't. Things had gone wrong, and he was the target for an entire community's animosity.

"Look, I'm sorry. I had no way of knowing that would happen."

She didn't look terribly mollified, and he didn't really expect her to be. The truth was he could have sold to his brother, but he'd erred on the side of money. The developers had offered more than he could turn down—enough to buy the dealership in the city free and clear.

And, yes, he'd harbored a few grudges against his perfect brother, Chet. This cattle drive was a favor to his brother, nothing more, and the last thing he needed was a distraction. He'd messed up and he didn't need a four-day-long reminder of that in the form of Dakota Mason, but Chet had asked her to lend a hand before Mackenzie's pregnancy troubles, and Andy was just filling Chet's shoes until he got back. This was all very temporary.

"Changed your mind about helping out?" Andy asked. "My brother isn't going to be back for a while, so you'd have to deal with me, whether you like it or not."

"Thanks to you, we need the extra money," she retorted. "So, no, I'm in."

Working with a woman who couldn't stand him was a bad idea. He knew that plain enough, but he couldn't shake the feeling he owed her. Just like the rest of this blasted town. He had a debt hanging over his head that he'd never be able to repay. Andy glanced at his watch. Two drovers had quit on

Chet, and they needed two replacements to get the job done. After Dakota, there was only one other applicant to the job posting he'd placed. He wasn't exactly in a position to turn down help.

"Have you done a cattle drive before?"

She shot him a sidelong look. "Are you seriously asking me that?"

It wasn't a completely inappropriate question. Andy hadn't gone on more than two cattle drives in his life. His brother had always been the one who cared about ranching operations—and was the consummate favorite—so their father had taken him along most years. Andy needed drovers who knew what they were doing, because while he was the face of the family for this drive, he didn't have the experience, and he knew it. Getting the job done was going to rely on the expertise of his team. Which brought up an important question.

"All the other drovers are men," he said. "Can you handle that?"

"If I can handle cattle, I can handle men." She narrowed her eyes. "Can *you* handle a woman on your team?"

Andy shot her a grin. He'd never been one to shy away from women. He'd managed to garner a bit of a reputation for himself over the years. In fact, he'd even dated his brother's wife back when they were in high school—and when he'd been dumb enough to cheat on her with another girl. Not his proudest moment. But while Hope might remember him as the flirt no one could nail down, the last few years had changed him in ways he'd mostly kept to himself. Seeing Chet and Mack fall in love, get married and now start a family made him realize what he wanted—the real thing.

"I have no problem working with a woman," he replied. "But if we're going to be working together for the next four days, maybe we could drop the personal vendetta. Like a truce."

She met his gaze without even a hint of a smile. "I can be professional."

Professional. Yeah, he'd had his fill of professional at the dealership. And if he had to spend the better part of a week with a group of people, he'd rather not feel their icy disapproval the entire time.

"I was actually aiming for friendly," he said and caught a flicker of humor in her direct gaze. "I'm not your favorite person, I get that. I hadn't realized how bad it was—" He swallowed, weighing his words. "You aren't the only one with a grudge around here. Do you know what it's like to order breakfast at the truck stop and have everyone there, including your waitress, glare at you? I think my eggs tasted funny, to boot. Goodness knows what they did to them. So I get it. I'm the bad guy. I'm the jerk who sold you all out, but I do have a job to do, and this isn't for me, it's for Chet."

Some of the tension in her shoulders loosened at the mention of his brother. That's the way it always was around here. People liked Chet. They respected him. They sided with him, too.

Her direct, cool expression didn't flicker. "I'll meet you halfway at civil."

"I'll take what I can get. If you want this job, we have to be able to work together. You know what it's like out there, and if we can't count on each other, we're wasting everyone's time."

"*I'm* not going to be your problem," she said, and he knew what she was talking about—the rest of the team.

"Leave the other guys to me." He wasn't exactly confident in his ability to lead this team of drovers, but if he could bridge the gap with Dakota, it would be a step in the right direction.

"So, what are the plans?" she asked.

"It's four days in total. I haven't done this particular ride before. It's to the far side of what used to be the Vaughn ranch. We're driving back four hundred head, so it's no small job."

Dakota nodded. "When do we start?"

"Monday morning."

"Okay, I'll be here bright and early." She rose to her feet and turned toward the door. Her jeans fit her nicely and he found himself having to pull his eyes away from admiring her shape.

"Dakota—"

"Yeah?" She turned back, brown eyes drilling into him, and he felt the urge to squirm.

This was the hard part—this was where he had to reveal that he needed help—and his stomach tightened. He didn't like admitting weakness, but needed an outside opinion, and she was the most qualified person in the room.

"You sold Chet some horses last spring," he said.

"What of it?" She raked a hand through her hair.

"I need to choose my horse for this drive, and I thought you might have some advice." More than advice. Dakota was something of a horse whisperer, able to calm even the most spirited animal, and while he knew she didn't much like him at the moment, he did trust her instincts. There was a horse he'd warmed up to over the last couple of days—Romeo. Chet thought Romeo wasn't ready for a cattle drive, but there was just something about that horse that Andy couldn't dismiss. Maybe he and Romeo were alike—not exactly ready but still perfectly capable. He wanted Dakota's take on it. Maybe she'd see something Chet hadn't.

When Dakota didn't answer right away, he added, "I know I'm not in the best position to ask you any personal favors, but it's been a long time since I worked a ranch, and Chet is counting on me to take care of things. Once I'm done this job, I'll go away and never bother you again. That's a promise."

She sighed. "Do you have time now? I'd need to see the horses again to see where they're at. They all needed work when they left my stables."

Andy shot her a grin and rose. "You bet. I have an hour until my interview with another potential drover."

"Who?" She frowned.

"Harley Webb. Heard of him?"

She shook her head. "No. He from around here?"

"Doesn't seem to be," he said. "I'll find out later, if he shows."

She gave him a curt nod and pulled open the door. There was something about this woman, her slim figure accentuated by morning sunlight, that made his mind stray into territory it didn't belong in. Just before that hazy summer, when Andy had dated Mackenzie, Dakota had started dating Andy's best friend, Dwight. She'd almost married him, so he'd seen quite a bit of Dakota back then. You'd think that would have made her more inclined to be friendly with him. But even back then she'd seen straight through his attempts to look tough and suave, and she hadn't liked what she'd seen. Now the woman had every reason to resent him; he had to keep that thought front and center.

Meanwhile he had a job to do. He'd do this cattle drive and, when Chet got back, he'd stay true to his word and get out of Hope for good. He'd celebrate Christmas in Billings and put all of this behind him. He'd seen enough over the last few days to be convinced that Hope would never be home sweet home again.

THE FACT THAT someone at the truck stop had meddled with Andy's morning eggs was mildly satisfying. He had it coming after what he'd done to this community, and he didn't deserve to swagger back into town and be welcomed with open arms. He'd formerly been a town favorite—up until he'd sold them all out. He'd been so cocksure of himself, and the girls had swooned for that auburn-hair-and-green-eyes combination—the Grangers were a good-looking family. It didn't help that Andy was a flirt, either, but Dakota had never been the kind of girl to be taken in by that kind of guy. She'd seen straight through him from the start.

Dakota respected substance over flattery, so after Andy broke about a dozen hearts around town after Mack's, and then up and sold his land to the developer, her sympathy—and everyone else's for that matter—was spent. Andy Granger was a flirt and an idiot. As for the scrambled eggs—whatever they'd done to them, he'd had it coming.

Andy walked half a step ahead of her across the ranch yard. A tractor hooked up to a trailer was parked along the western fence, a few bales of hay and some tools on the trailer bed. Several goats were in the field beyond it, and they bleated in greeting as they passed. A chicken coop sat at the far end of the yard by the big, red barn and a rooster perched on a fence post nearby fluffed his feathers against the chill. A few hens scratched in the dirt outside the coop, but it looked like most had gone inside for some cozy comfort.

Andy angled his steps around the coop and Dakota noted how broad and strong he was still. City life hadn't softened him physically. It had been almost five years since she'd last clapped eyes on him, and she'd forgotten how attractive he was up close... Not that it mattered.

A breeze picked up, swirling some leaves across their path, and she hitched her shoulders against the probing wind.

Word had spread about Andy, even when he was away. He'd spent a decade in the city, where he'd gotten engaged and then got cold feet, from what she'd heard through the grapevine. Then he'd sold the Granger pasture and left town again. It would have taken some courage to show his face after all that, but here he was, and he was doing this for his brother, which was the only reason she was being helpful at all—well, that and the money.

Dakota had known Andy quite well back in the day. He'd even asked her out once, leaning against the hood of his pickup and casting her a boyish grin. Truthfully, she'd been tempted to say yes—what girl hadn't? But she'd just started dating Dwight and she wasn't the two-timing kind of person. And what kind of a guy moved in on his best friend's girlfriend? She'd turned him down flat, which was just as well because a few weeks later Mackenzie Granger came to town and soon they were a smoldering item. That just went to show that the boyish grin wasn't to be trusted.

Ironically enough, Andy turned out to be less of a threat to her peace of mind than Dwight had been. The minute Dwight turned twenty-one, he did two things: propose and start drinking. She accepted his proposal, but the wedding never happened. With the booze, Dwight got violent, and she couldn't stay in a relationship like that. Still, canceling her wedding had been the hardest thing she'd ever done. And Andy had been Dwight's best friend—it said something about the kind of man Andy was, in her estimation. Birds of a feather and all that.

"So your eggs tasted funny, did they?" she asked, casting him a wry smile.

Andy shook his head. "You know, in a place this small you get to know everybody, but you also get to tick everybody off in one fell swoop, too."

"So why come back?" she countered. "I've heard that you're set up pretty well in Billings, and while I get helping out your brother, Elliot could have led this drive easily enough."

In fact, she'd heard that Andy was rich, if she had to be entirely honest. Apparently he was making money hand over fist in the city, which was one more reason for people around here to resent him. It was easier to feel sorry for a guy who ended up down on his luck after pulling a stunt like that, but to have him actually prosper…

"I am set up pretty well." His tone became more guarded and he looked away for a moment. "Let's just say that some sentimental nonsense got the better of me."

"Is that code for a woman?" she asked dryly. With Andy it usually came down to a woman.

"No." He barked out a laugh. "Is that what you think of me, that I'm some kind of womanizer?"

Dakota shrugged. She couldn't see any reason to lie. He had to know his own reputation. "Yes."

He eyed her for a moment as if not sure how to take her frankness, then he shrugged.

"Well, this particular sentimental nonsense has nothing to do with a woman. This is about my dad, rest his soul, and my brother. I guess I missed…them. This. Fitting in. Like I said, nonsense. There is no turning back that clock."

She didn't miss the fact that he hadn't exactly denied being a womanizer, but she did feel a little pang of pity at the mention of his father. Mr. Granger had died about four years earlier in a tractor accident. The whole town had showed up for the funeral. Even the truck stop closed down for a couple of hours so that everyone could attend; that's how loved Andy's father had been. She inwardly grimaced.

"I didn't send the horses out to pasture today," Andy went on, saving her from finding an appropriate reply.

He led the way around the side of the newly painted barn toward the corral. As they stepped into its shadow, the December day felt distinctly colder. This winter would make up for lost time; there was no doubt about it.

Andy glanced over his shoulder and his green eyes met hers. "Thanks for this, by the way."

Her pulse sped up at the directness of that look and the very fact that he was working his blasted Granger charm on her was irritating.

"This isn't for you, Granger. It's for Chet."

She wasn't falling for any of Andy's charms, but she could certainly understand why some women did. He was tall, muscular, with rugged good looks and scruff on his face that suggested he'd missed a couple of days of shaving. But Andy also represented something that hit her a little closer to home—the kind of guy who could walk away without too much trouble. Her brother had fallen for the female version of Andy Granger in the form of Nina Harpe, and she wasn't about to repeat Brody's mistakes. She had a lot of reasons to be wary of Andy Granger.

The corral was attached to the back of the barn, bathed in midmorning sunlight. At this time of year the sunlight was watery, but the air was surprisingly warm—about four or five degrees above freezing. Beyond the corral was a dirt road that lead toward different enclosed pastures, rolling hills of rich, golden cinnamon grass glowing in late autumn splendor. And beyond the fields were the mountains, rising in jagged peaks, hemming them in like majestic guards.

Several horses perked up at the sight of them, ears twitching in interest. Andy reached into a white bucket that sat in the shade and pulled out a fistful of carrots. He rolled them over in his hands, rubbing off the last of the dirt, and headed for the fence. Two of the horses came right over when Andy walked up—a dun stallion named Romeo and a piebald mare. Chet's horse, a chestnut gelding named Barney, stood resolutely on the far side of the coral, ignoring them.

"Have you ridden any of them yet?" Dakota

asked, stopping at Andy's side. He held a carrot out to the mare.

"I've ridden Romeo, here," he said, reaching out to pet the stallion's nose. Romeo leaned closer, nosing for a carrot, and Andy obliged.

"How about Barney?" she asked, nodding toward the gelding that was inching closer around the side of the corral, wanting his own share of the treats.

"He bit me," Andy retorted.

Dakota choked back a laugh. "Not sweet old Barney."

"Sweet?" Andy shook his head. "That horse hates me. Every chance he gets, he gives me a nip. I just about lost the top of my ear last time."

"Okay, well, not Barney, then," she replied with a shake of her head. In fact, if Andy wasn't going to ride Barney, she was inclined to take him herself. He was an experienced horse for this ride, a sweetheart deep down…if you weren't Andy, apparently.

"So what do you think?" he asked.

She paused for a moment, considering.

"Romeo, here, is young and strong. He's a runner. He'll go and go, so he'll definitely have the energy for a cattle drive. But he doesn't have the experience."

"I like him, though," Andy said. Romeo crunched another carrot, his jaw grinding in slow, satisfied circles. "He wasn't Chet's first choice, either."

"Which horse did Chet recommend?" she asked.

"Patty," he said, nodding to the piebald mare. "But what do you think?"

Dakota looked over the horses. "I'd have said Barney, but if he really hates you that much—"

"And he does," Andy replied in a low laugh.

"Patty is a good horse. She'd do well." She paused, watching the way Romeo stretched toward Andy for another carrot. "But you seem to have a good bond with Romeo. I don't know. I'd say it's between Patty and Romeo. Patty would be my first choice. I think Romeo's a risk."

Andy nodded. "Thanks. I appreciate it." He gave the last carrot to Patty and showed Romeo his empty hands. "Sorry, buddy. All out."

Andy pushed himself off the fence and Dakota followed him as he headed back the way they'd come. Sunlight warmed her shoulders and the top of her head. She glanced around the yard as they walked, inhaling the comforting scent of hay and autumn chill.

"So?" she prodded.

"When have I ever been one to take good advice?" he asked with a grin. "I'm taking Romeo. If I'm going to ride for four days, I'd rather have it be with a horse that wants to move."

Somehow this didn't surprise her in the least, and not in a pleasant way. Andy Granger had always made his own rules. "Fair enough."

"What?" He cast her a quizzical look.

"Did you really want my advice, or just a vote for what you already wanted to do?"

"Hey." His tone grew deeper and his eyes met

hers. "I might not be the rancher of the family, but I'm not exactly a lost kitten, either. I can ride."

Dakota dropped her gaze, her cheeks warming. Andy had an effective stare.

"I grew up here, too, you know," he added. His stride was long and she had to pick up her pace to keep up with him.

He may have grown up in Hope, but she knew he'd never taken ranching very seriously.

"You clowned around," she retorted. "I remember that horse show where you arrived late and—"

"I had my fun," he interrupted. "And why not? No one else took me seriously."

"They might have," she shot back, "if you'd shown that you cared about this land at all."

"And if I were punctual." He gave her a look of mock seriousness. "So very punctual."

He was making fun of her now and she shook her head. Andy had been late for that horse show, and she'd told him off for it when he finally did arrive. It was that joking attitude of his that rubbed her the wrong way—it always had. Always joking, never saying anything of any substance. In her own humble opinion, Andy's father had made the right call in who got the ranch.

"You were late, and I came in first at that show," she said. She'd enjoyed beating him.

"I was late and I still came in third," he quipped. "Imagine what I could've done if I'd arrived on time."

"Yes," she retorted. "Imagine."

The thing was Andy hadn't lacked in skill or talent, just focus. At least that was the way she saw it. And he hadn't focused because he hadn't cared about ranching life. But Dakota did—she cared more than a guy like Andy could ever imagine, and while he was horsing around and flirting with girls, she'd been working hard. It wasn't just a junior horse show, it was a matter of pride.

"I was joking." He came to a stop in front of the house and shoved his hands into his pockets. He didn't sober entirely, that smile still teasing at the corners of his mouth. "You'll get used to it."

From where they stood she could see the barn on one side and the drive leading toward the main road on the other. It wound through bushes of amber and nut brown, a few cattails growing in the ditch where water collected. The cluck of the chickens mingled with the faraway call of a lone V of geese that soared overhead. She could see the beauty here—the life, the rotation of the seasons, the work to be done and the harvest to be enjoyed. She could see things she was quite sure Andy didn't. The land wasn't a joke, it was a responsibility.

"I'm already used to it," she retorted. "You're acting like I don't know you. If you want to know why people are so ticked with you, this is it. This is all a joke for you, just a way to pass the time. But for the rest of us, this is our life, something we care enough about to dedicate every waking hour. When you sold that land, you made a dent in this community and it's affected us all—my family especially. You might be joking around, but the rest of us are dead serious, and we're left paying for it."

"And I doubt there's any way you'll forgive me, is there?" He'd sobered finally, the joking look evaporating from his face, leaving those chiseled Granger good looks to drill straight into her.

"Probably not." Dakota sucked in a breath and nodded in the direction of the corral. "I still recommend Patty, for the record. Not that I expect it to matter to you."

"Noted. And I should add that just because I joke around doesn't mean I'm not dead serious about some things, this cattle drive included."

"Good." She swallowed, uncertain of what else to say. There was nothing left, really. She'd stated her position and he'd stated his. They weren't friends. They weren't anything, really, except two people forced to work together for a few days. What he thought of this land didn't much matter. It didn't belong to him.

"So I'll see you Monday morning," he said. "I want to start riding at sunup."

"I'll see you then," she said and turned toward her truck.

"Dakota—" She turned back and he shrugged. "Thanks for meeting me halfway."

Halfway at civil. It wasn't much, but it seemed to mean something to him. Melancholy swam in those green eyes and then he gave her a nod of farewell and turned back toward the house. For all of his joking around, he was carrying a heavier load than she'd given him credit for. While she'd always hoped he'd live to regret what he'd done to this town by selling out, she'd never considered what it would mean to see that regret reflected in his face. Karma was best reported secondhand, not witnessed…something she'd already learned with Dwight.

A few years ago, right around Christmastime, she remembered putting up the family tree in the living room with her brother. She'd been dating Dwight at the time, and no one knew about his violent outburst yet, but apparently, his boozing had put up some warning flags. Brody had given her some sound advice. "Don't get caught up with a guy who will ruin your future," he'd told her seriously. "You already know what you want. Dwight doesn't—and even if he did, he'd have to stop drinking if he wanted to achieve anything. So you'd better put together the life you want. No guy is going to give it to you, least of all Dwight. You need to dump his sorry butt before it's too late."

That advice still applied—both about steering clear of Dwight and any other guy who didn't share her priorities. The wrong man could demolish everything she'd worked for.

Chapter Two

Dakota put her truck into reverse and pulled a three-point turn before heading out the drive that lead to the main road. She steered around a pothole, the dried fingertips of bushes scratching across the side of her vehicle. Mission accomplished: she'd secured the job. When Chet had called several days ago asking her to lend a hand on their late cattle drive for a decent sum, she'd been relieved. They needed the extra money rather badly, especially with Christmas coming up. Sometimes blessings came in the form of hard work.

Andy had been a surprise, though.

She turned onto the main road and heaved a sigh. She'd been more nervous than she'd thought when she realized she'd be dealing with Andy and not his more likeable brother. But a job was a job, and with her mother's medical bills for her emergency hysterectomy last year and the down payment they needed to put down for the new hydration system, she'd take a paycheck any way she could get it, and this drover position was paying relatively well. Chet was like that. He knew better than to offer the Masons charity, but he'd offer a job for fair pay. That was the sort of kindness Dakota could accept.

The road divided the land—one side an endless, rippling carpet of golden wheat, the other what used to be the Granger's pasture, a mixture of maize yellow with olive green and sienna—the different grasses maturing together into a rich expanse, the beauty of which was marred by muddy roads. The growl of large machinery surfed the breeze, tractors creeping along the ground in the distance, and every time she looked at them, a new wave of anger swept over her. Lordship Land Developers had friends in powerful places to get the zoning for this eyesore, and all the petitions she'd filed had made no difference at all. Apparently money spoke louder than righteous indignation. And Dakota had plenty of righteous indignation.

This county—this road—was as much a part of her as her own blood, and seeing it torn apart hurt on a gut level. Andy had seemed properly surprised at the impact his choice had had on their ranch, but it didn't change where the blame lay. He'd had one foot out of town for as long as she'd known him. Again, a lot like Nina Harpe—the woman engaged to her brother, Brody…whom her brother still believed he'd marry. Except, Nina had up and married Brody's best friend while he was stationed overseas with the army. Nina was more than beautiful—she was voluptuous and sexy, a Marilyn Monroe singing

Happy Birthday to the president. Apparently, one of her virtues wasn't patience.

Dakota wasn't given to petty grudges. She believed in second chances and people's ability to grow, unless that person had singlehandedly impoverished her family's land or broken her brother's heart. Her benevolence had a limit. To be fair, Brody's heart wasn't broken yet…but that clock was ticking.

And yet, in one small corner of her own heart, she found herself pitying Andy. He deserved what he got—there was no ambivalence there—yet the softer side of her still hated to see someone suffer. Even Andy Granger.

A few miles farther led to her own drive and she slowed to make the turn. As her tires crunched over the gravel, her phone chirped on the seat beside her. It was an incoming email. She glanced down and saw that it was from Brody. It was always a treat to hear from him, except lately, when he was asking more persistently about Nina. There was more to that story and she couldn't be the one to tell him.

Dakota and Brody always had been close as kids. She'd been fiercely protective of her quiet big brother, and he'd never really treated her like a little kid. Before he'd left, they'd discussed the future of the ranch in depth together, and it felt weird to have him so far away. But this was what Brody had always dreamed of, joining the army and protecting his country.

A brown, floppy-eared mutt raced after the truck as she pulled to a stop next to the single-level ranch house. Shelby bounced excitedly, planting several muddy footprints into Dakota's jeans when she opened the door.

"Hi, girl," she said, scratching the dog behind the ears.

"That you, Dakota?" Her mother's voice came from the house and then she appeared at the screen door. Her sweater was rolled up to the elbows, her front covered in a floral print apron and her hands— held up like a surgeon's—were covered in flour.

"Hi, Mom."

"Where were you?"

"I was just lining things up with the Grangers for their cattle drive." Dakota gave Shelby another rub and then headed toward the house. She kicked her boots against the step on her way in.

She glanced down at her phone and skimmed her brother's email as she came in past the screen door.

"What are you reading?" her mother asked, glancing over her shoulder. She was working on some cinnamon buns, rolling out the fluffy dough with a heavy, wooden rolling pin.

"Email from Brody."

"How's he doing?"

They all missed Brody. He'd been gone a full year now, and anyone who heard from him was honor-bound to share with the rest of the family. He was serving the country, and Dakota was so proud of him it almost hurt sometimes, but that only made their secret here at home all the heavier.

"He's asking about Nina again," Dakota said as

she came into the kitchen, and she and her mother exchanged a look.

"What did you say?" her mother asked, reaching for the butter plate.

"I haven't answered him." Dakota sighed. "I really don't like lying to him, Mom. He's going to hate us for this."

Brody was the big, burly kind of guy who kept his thoughts to himself, but that didn't mean he didn't feel things deeply. Dakota had often thought the girl who ended up with her brother would be lucky, indeed, which was why his choice of Nina Harpe had been such a disappointment. But he'd asked Nina to marry him and she'd accepted. What could they do?

"I don't want him distracted over that little idiot when he's dodging bullets," she retorted. *That little idiot* was what her mother had called Nina since she'd sheepishly announced she was marrying Brian Dickerson eight months after Brody had been deployed. She'd followed through with that—a tiny wedding she'd agreed to keep secret—and then promptly moved to the city with her new husband. To add insult to injury, Brian had been Brody's best friend since elementary school. They both were going to have some explaining to do when Brody got back home. As was Dakota when she'd have to tell her brother why she'd kept the secret, and she wasn't looking forward to coming clean. Brody was going to be crushed.

Brody was better off without Nina, though. She was flighty and more preoccupied with material objects and celebrity gossip than she was anything worthwhile. She had perfectly coiffed red hair, swaying hips and breasts like melons. She left a cloud of perfume in her wake, and a string of gaping men.

Nina was a self-involved flirt, much like Andy Granger, but having Nina take up with Brian behind her brother's back was worse. Brody's taste might be a little lacking, but he deserved better than that while he fought for his country. Apparently, Nina hadn't been able to wait long before she got sidetracked by the next available guy. They'd all agreed to keep the secret until he got back. Then Nina could rip his heart out at her leisure, when he was safely home again.

"Don't worry, I have plenty to distract Brody with," Dakota said with a wry smile. "Did you know that Chet and Mackenzie are at the city hospital right now?"

"I just heard that from Audrey," her mother said with a frown. "Apparently the babies are low in amniotic fluid and she needs to be under medical supervision. Who's taking care of the ranch while they're gone?"

"Andy."

"What?" Her mother looked back. "Seriously? So the prodigal son has come back, has he?"

"As a favor to Chet, he claims," she replied, her mind flashing to the meeting at the Granger ranch. "So he'll be the one leading the cattle drive. I don't think Andy knows enough to lead one on his own, but apparently he's going to try."

Her mother fell silent and they exchanged a tired look. Andy Granger was old news. They'd talked about him on a regular basis, and he'd grown bigger and badder with each mention.

Dakota remembered coming back late one night after the construction had started and the water had dried up, and could recall overhearing her parents talking in the kitchen, their voices filtering through the open window. Her father had sounded so gutted, so deeply sad, that his deep voice trembled.

"Millie, we might lose this place…" There had been a pause so long Dakota's leg had almost cramped as she'd tried to stay still. "That Granger kid… He did this. I don't think I'll ever forgive him."

Dakota had never forgotten those words or the quivering sadness in his voice. Because of Andy, her father stood to lose the land that fueled his heart, and she was determined to do whatever it took to keep them ranching.

Hence looking for side work and extra income. She'd taken anything she could get for the last several years, but it had never quite added up to enough.

"The cattle drive starts Monday," Dakota said. "So, like I said, I'll have plenty to update Brody about without having to say much of anything about Nina."

"Are you sure you want to do this?" her mother asked. "You agreed to work with Chet, not Andy."

"There aren't that many jobs posted right now, Mom." Dakota picked up an apple from the fruit bowl and polished it on her shirt. "And the Grangers are

paying pretty well. Don't worry. I can deal with Andy
Granger for a few days." Dakota shot her mother a
grin. "I'm pretty sure he's more afraid of me than I
am of him."

Her bravado was only partially sincere, though.
She wasn't looking forward in the least to doing a
cattle drive with Andy, but the last thing her mother
needed was to shoulder more guilt about the family
finances. It wasn't her fault that she'd gotten sick or
that the insurance company had fallen through when
they'd needed them most. What mattered was that
she'd gotten the hysterectomy she'd so desperately
needed and was back to full strength.

"As for Nina…" her mother added. "We only have
to keep the secret until your brother gets home in
February. Just a few months longer. I'd rather have
him find out when he has family support."

It was an old conversation—one they'd had a hundred times before—and Dakota stared down at the
polished apple in her hands.

"What about Dad?" she asked cautiously. "I know
how he feels about Andy and all—"

"He'll be fine. A paycheck is a paycheck." She
smiled wanly. "As long as you think you can handle it."

Dakota took a bite of the crisp apple and chewed
thoughtfully. Times like these she missed her brother
the most. Brody would have some wisecrack to make
them laugh and he'd manage to cut Andy down to
size in no time.

"I'm going to go fill the feeders before it gets too

late," Dakota said. They'd done their own cattle drive last month and the whole herd was back in the nearby fields. The cows wouldn't wait, and she still had to sort out how they'd manage the work while she was gone for a few days. There was one thing she wanted more than anything else, and that was to ranch this very land she was raised on, if only she could get her father to let go of his hopes for Brody taking it over. She glanced down at her brother's email.

Is Nina okay? She seems distant, but I guess I'm a bit distant, too. I want to do the right thing and marry her when I get back. I know you don't like frilly stuff, but any chance you'd pitch in and help to put together a wedding?

This family was in tatters; their finances were shaky. Right about now, doing a cattle drive with the man who'd dried up their land didn't seem half bad compared to facing the rest of their problems.

She needed a paycheck. She'd start with that.

HARLEY WEBB ARRIVED on time with a cigarette behind his ear and a worn New Testament tucked into the front pocket of his fleece-lined jean jacket. He looked young—too young for this job. He'd barely grown a mustache and the rest of his face looked smooth as a boy's. A cowboy hat sat firmly on his head and his hands looked too big for his wiry physique, like an overgrown puppy. So this was the bottom of the barrel, apparently.

"Harley, I take it?" Andy asked, shaking the kid's calloused hand—at least he'd done some hard work in his life.

"That's right," Harley replied. "Good to meet you."

While Dakota had the unpleasant surprise of seeing Andy instead of Chet, Andy had been the one to call Harley for an interview, and it was mildly relieving not to have to explain his presence to someone. That being said, he didn't know this kid from Adam, and he was used to having some sort of personal association with the men who worked the ranch—either they'd worked on a neighboring ranch in the past or were related to someone from the county. Harley, however, seemed to have dropped down from above—a gangly, questionable gift.

"So where are you from?" Andy asked, leading the way into the house.

"Idaho," he replied.

"And what brings you here?" Andy stood back while Harley came inside. He gestured to a kitchen chair and both men sat. Harley took off his hat, his thin, brown hair flattened against his forehead.

"I came out here to visit some family," Harley said. He fiddled with the edge of his hat. "Decided to stay a bit longer, and I need to make some money."

Andy nodded. It sounded plausible. "How old are you?"

"Twenty-two." Harley laughed self-consciously. "Trust me, I get carded a lot."

"You have some ID?" Andy asked, and Harley shrugged, leaned the side and pried a wallet out of his back pocket. His Idaho driver's license confirmed his age.

Andy handed it back. "All right. So let's talk experience, then."

"I was raised on a ranch," Harley said. "I've done it all. I can rope, herd, brand—you name it. I've done cattle drives before."

He sounded confident enough—and today was Saturday. There wasn't much time to find another drover if he didn't take Harley.

"You know anyone around here who can vouch for you?" Andy asked. "You said you're visiting family. Who are they?"

"My sister—her name is Holly Webb. She lives in town here."

That didn't help. He'd never heard of her. "Anyone else?"

"Sorry." Harley shook his head. "But I'll work hard. You can count on that. I'm honest and I'll earn my keep."

Andy paused, considering. Hiring someone at the car dealership was different, since he had a human resources official to check into work histories and the like. He had no way of checking out Harley's story on such short notice. This one was left up to his gut. The way he saw it right now, they could ride with Harley or without him. Even if he wasn't much of a drover, he'd be an extra body for night watches. That was something. On the bright side, he might be as good as he claimed. Besides, he'd showed up on time and, despite Andy's teasing of Dakota earlier, he did value punctuality in his employees; it showed the kid wanted the job.

"Okay, well, this is what we offer." Andy wrote a number on a slip of paper and slid it across the table. "That's not negotiable."

"Looks fair, sir," Harley replied with a nod.

"If you want the job, you're hired," Andy said. "We start out Monday at sunup. Be here an hour early and we'll get you fitted with a horse. I'll need a copy of your ID..."

The next few minutes were filled with legalities and forms. There was something about Harley that Andy liked. Maybe it was that Harley was oblivious to Andy's past and only seemed to relate to him as a boss and source of a potential paycheck. Call it vanity, but it felt good to be called "sir" again instead of the other, less flattering descriptions he'd overheard. Ordinarily he'd be more cautious about an unknown ranch hand, but lately he was a little more sympathetic toward people wanting a fresh start. They weren't so easy to achieve and he envied those who managed it.

Plus, with Christmas coming up, he was more sentimental than usual. Christmas was hard—it had been ever since his mother had passed away right around the holiday when he was thirteen. Christmases were never the same without her. It wasn't anything concrete like her cookies or the way she always found the perfect gift for the people she loved... it was her. Without Mom, it was like the sun dimmed and the moon went out. Those were some of the memories he hoped to escape when he left Hope after this cattle drive. Christmas needed to be in Billings this year—in his modern apartment with his new life. He couldn't face another Christmas in Hope.

After Harley left, Andy took the paperwork into the office. He pulled out a fresh file folder and grabbed a ballpoint to write out the newest employee's name. Andy wasn't quite the lackadaisical jokester that Dakota took him for, but her assumptions weren't her fault. He'd worked for that reputation out of a deep sense of hurt and betrayal. He wasn't a guy who liked to advertise his vulnerability because, ironically enough, even though he'd put his teenage energy into proving he didn't care, the thing he'd wanted most from the people in his community was their respect. Maybe even a "sir" now and again.

But that was long gone.

When he was a kid, his brother and his dad would go out to check on the cattle. Andy used to go with them, but he felt the inequality in how they were treated. Chet was his dad's favorite, the one he talked to when he was explaining how something worked. Andy was just along for the ride—or that was how it felt. He was treated like a little kid, even though he was only two years younger than Chet, and when he told jokes, his dad would say, "Enough," and the growl in his voice said it all. Mom wasn't like that, though. When Andy told her a joke, she'd throw back her head and laugh.

She also made an amazing blueberry pie.

He'd never be like his stoic father, but he wanted

a woman like his mom—full of love and laughter, who stood by her man through thick and thin. If there was one thing about Mom, she was loyal. Even when the laughter stopped and her eyes turned sad, she was still loyal.

He tucked the photocopies of Harley's ID and his signed contract into the file folder. He dropped it in the back of the employee section of the file cabinet the way Chet had organized it.

Andy turned off the light on his way out of the office. For some reason an image of Dakota kept rising in his mind when he thought about what he wanted in life, and it was like his subconscious was taunting him. Dakota was the one woman who never would fall for his charms. She never had. In fact, she was the woman with the biggest grudge against him.

And yet there was something about the way her eyes snapped fire when she'd stood there in the driveway, cheeks pink from the chilly wind and a thumb hooked in her belt loop... *If you want to know why people are so ticked with you, this is it.*

Apparently he was a sucker for punishment. He'd come back to help out Chet in his time of need, and that was where it was supposed to stop. He'd known full well it would be hard. He'd known he'd have to deal with some painful memories. He'd even known he'd be resented. He just hadn't counted on feeling this attracted to the one woman who resented him most.

Andy pushed the thought aside and grabbed his hat off the table where he'd tossed it. There were chores to be done, animals to check on... He had enough to worry about for the next week or so. Keeping his mind on his job was the best solution he could think of.

Chapter Three

Monday morning, the sun was just peeping over the horizon as Andy cinched the girth on his saddle tighter. Early rays of sunlight, pink as a grapefruit, flooded the fields, sparkling on the frost that clung to every blade of grass. Dawn made the ranch cozier somehow. It was the rose-splashed sky and the long, dusty shadows—a moment in time that hadn't changed over the years. He could remember this exact moment of the day when he was a kid holding a bucket of chicken feed, staring at the sky.

"Get 'er done, Andy," his father would say on his way past, Chet in his wake. Get 'er done. Staring at the dawn wasn't efficient use of his time, but it was something his mom could understand.

"Just look at that sky…" She'd stare at the sky for long moments. Mom got it.

The rooster let out a hoarse crow and Romeo stamped a hoof as Andy ran a hand down the horse's dun flank. His team consisted of four regular ranch hands who rode along for cattle drives every year, and the two newbies—Harley Webb and Dakota Mason.

Dakota was getting Barney ready to ride a few yards off. She slid a feedbag over his head and patted his neck affectionately. Andy found it ironic she'd chosen Chet's horse, the beast that kept nipping at Andy every time he came close. He looked gentle as a lamb with Dakota, though.

The sunrise made her milky skin flush pink in the growing light, her dark hair pulled into a ponytail, revealing the length of her neck. Her coat was brown leather, tough and formfitting, and he had to force himself to look away. Staring, no matter how flattering the light, was bad form for the boss.

Andy's last cattle drive had been when he was sixteen, and he was more than aware of his current limitations—namely, his lack of recent ranching experience and his mangled reputation in Hope. Drovers were a unique lot and gaining their respect wouldn't be automatic, maybe not even possible given his current position. These were hard-riding men who were used to discomfort and had their own code, and leadership on a cattle drive would look a whole lot different than leadership in a boardroom.

Harley seemed to be keeping to himself and a couple of the other drovers were talking by the fence. Dakota buckled shut a saddlebag and glanced in his direction, her hat pushed back from her face while she worked. She was pretty in a way he didn't see very often. She wasn't Cover Girl pretty. It was something deeper; the way she stared directly at a man and he could see both the softness and sharp intelligence behind those eyes, an alluring combination. He didn't want a woman to look up to him, bat her eyes and laugh at his jokes. He wanted a woman to match him, and something told him that if she were properly invested, Dakota absolutely could.

The sun rose steadily higher in the sky, the light turning from rosy to golden. Dakota's fingers moved with the nimble deftness of experience. Her voice was low as she said something to the horse, her words lost in the few yards between them. Andy had meant to stay away, but he couldn't hold himself back any longer.

"You have enough food for the day?" Andy asked, heading in her direction. The cook would meet them at the first camp, but until they arrived they were responsible for carrying their own food. It was a question at least.

"I've done this before." She put a hand on her hip. "I'd check on the little guy, if I were you."

She nodded in Harley's direction. He and Elliot, the most experienced ranch hand the Granger's employed, were eyeing each other distrustfully from where they sat in their saddles. That didn't look promising.

"What's up with them?" Andy asked, keeping his tone low enough for privacy.

Dakota shrugged. "Don't like each other by the looks of it."

He laughed softly. "Yeah, I picked up on that."

"You sure about that horse?" she asked, nodding in Romeo's direction.

"You don't think I know what I'm doing, do you?" he asked. She wouldn't be alone in the opinion—his dad and brother had thought the same.

"I'm better at this than you are."

Her tone held challenge and she was probably right. He was no drover, he was a businessman, and while he was excellent at making a profit and driving up the value of shares, cattle and drovers weren't part of his expertise. Not anymore, at least.

"You may very well be," he said, shooting her a grin. "But I'm a quick study."

He didn't know why he felt the need to compete with her. It shouldn't matter, but he didn't want her to see him as weak or needing her help. This might be temporary, but he was still in charge until his brother got back. She'd offered to meet him halfway at civil, but he was aiming at a whole lot more than that. He wanted her respect, but that would have to be earned.

"We'll see."

Andy shot her a rueful grin and headed back to his horse. He put his boot in the stirrup and grabbed the horn, swinging himself up into his saddle. He looked around at the team he'd be riding with, and he could see that they were solid in experience, if not all entirely friendly. Harley's New Testament was still tucked into the front pocket of his jacket and he chewed on the inside of his cheek. Behind him, Elliot Sturgeon stared hard at a point just left of Andy, his reins held in a loose grip. He was good at his job and could have led this cattle drive. He wasn't Andy's biggest fan, either, which made this prickly.

"Okay," Andy said, raising his voice over another hoarse crow from the rooster sitting on the fence rail next to the henhouse. "So I think we're all pretty clear on our route. We're heading due west for about a day and a half. We've got some newbies this time, so let's not assume everyone knows everything—"

"Like you…" a low, gravelly voice said, and Andy glanced in the direction the voice had originated, only to see three drovers eyeing him with the same bland expression. It wasn't worth the confrontation right now, but he could see they didn't respect him. That could turn ugly a couple hours past civilization. He needed to address this now and a couple of different ideas flitted through his head before he settled on the words.

"I've never done this route, but I'm here because this is my family's herd," he said, keeping his voice even, and he let his gaze move over his team slowly. "You might like me and you might not. I might like you and I might not. Anyone who figures four days with me ain't worth the money, drop out now and save me the aggravation. Anyone who makes trouble on this trip can expect a pink slip when we get back. No exceptions."

No one moved, and a horse snorted. The drovers looked down, except for Harley, who looked straight at Andy, nothing against him yet, apparently. Dakota's gaze didn't drop, either, but her expression hadn't exactly softened. Romeo started to prance in place, and Andy tightened his hold on the reins.

"Good. I take that to mean you're all in. You're here because Chet wanted you here or because I hired you. You're all good at what you do, and we can make this a smooth ride. Let's review the route."

They'd ride to the first camp at Loggerhead Creek, where the cooks would be waiting. The cooks this year were Andy's uncle and aunt, and they'd drive a horse trailer over with two pack horses. The next morning Andy and the drovers would set out for the foothills where the cattle were grazing. They'd take the pack horses with them to carry the kit they needed for their next camp. They'd cross the Hell Bent River, which lived up to its name during spring runoff, and they'd round up the cattle and camp there for the second night. Then they'd drive them back. They'd stop once more at Loggerhead Creek, where they'd camp again, drop off the pack horses, and then carry enough food with them to drive the cattle home. Four days. It was a pretty smooth operation. Chet had worked out the kinks in the last three years since his marriage.

"Any questions?" Andy asked, looking over the group, the morning sun shining at their backs so that he had to squint. No one broke the silence, so Andy gave a curt nod. "Let's go."

He pulled Romeo around. The other drovers kicked their horses into motion and they all set out at a brisk canter toward the western pasture. Andy hung back and then took up the rear. His earlier bravado was starting to wane and he glanced over his shoulder, back at the ranch.

He remembered the last cattle drive he'd done with his dad and brother. Riding out with the drovers had seemed like an adventure, except that his father had always talked more seriously with Chet. He'd ask Chet's opinion; suggest different ways Chet could look at things. Chet got advice and Andy got criticism. He'd treated Chet like the heir and Andy was more like a visitor along for the fun of the drive.

Keep out of the way, Andy. Your brother has this one.

Andy, you're going to get yourself kicked in the head if you keep that up!

Andy, why don't you go start supper? We'll take care of the rest out here...

It had always been like that. Chet and Dad had a kind of bond Andy couldn't explain or share. They were alike—serious, quiet and immovable. Andy, on the other hand, had laughed louder and filled those silences his brother and father left hanging out in the stillness. And now, as a grown man, he felt the resurgence of adolescent angst. Andy had been better at ranch work than his father ever knew because, frankly, his father never stopped to notice.

Elliot dismounted and opened the gate that led into the pasture. The fence stretched out across the rolling field, shrinking and blurring into the distance until it dropped out of sight down a steep grade on one side and climbed the rolling incline on the other. A fence was a constant source of upkeep for a rancher, and Andy could appreciate the sight of a well-maintained one. The gate opened with a groan and when they'd all filed through, Elliot closed it again with the thump of metal against wooden post, fastening the latch.

The pasture opened up ahead of them, the grass rippling in a cold wind that cut across the plains with nothing to stop it. The snow might be late this year, but it would come, and overhead there was another honking V of geese moving south. Andy kicked Romeo into motion and the drovers fanned out, each taking some space as they rode.

He'd known on that last cattle drive that none of it would change. Ever. It was on horseback with the drovers that Andy had decided to make his own life and his own future away from the land he'd grown up on. Andy loved the land, too—or he had until he'd realized that it would never be his. But while his brother loved the very soil under his boots, Andy had loved the horizon—that tickle of land meeting sky, so full of possibility. He loved the disappearing line of fence as it dwindled into the distance, and the gentle touch of pink along the horizon as the sun crept slowly upward. He liked clouds that soared like battleships, leaving dark shadows beneath them, and the whistle of wind past his face as he rode at full gallop. The soil was good, but the horizon was better. He might be pushed out of the ranch, but that didn't push him out of life. Sometimes, it was best not to get attached to something never intended for you anyway.

Andy found himself watching Dakota from the

corner of his eye as she slowly overtook him. She was an experienced rider and her attention appeared to be on the scenery around them. A glowing sunrise and frost melting into dew as far the sunbeams stretched. She blended into the moment seamlessly, a cowgirl cantering across the pasture, and Andy sucked in a chilled breath of morning air. He'd do well to keep his focus off the backside of Dakota Mason—she was another one never meant for the likes of him.

Watching his team riding, horse strides lengthening into a comfortable gate, riders settling into the motion, he felt that same sense of disconnect he'd felt all those years ago—he was an outsider here. But looking at Dakota ride, her ponytail bouncing on her back, her hips moving with the horse underneath her, he felt a different kind of longing. This Montana land wasn't his and it never would be, but if he could belong anywhere, he wanted it to be with a woman like Dakota. Dwight had never deserved her, and maybe Andy didn't, either, but he'd have at least treated her right.

But that had been a long time ago—too long ago to even matter now that they were all adults. He'd felt a twinge of that when he'd seen Mackenzie again four years ago. She'd reminded him of what he wanted most, too, but that had been more of a nostalgic shiver, a realization that he'd been an idiot way back then. Looking at Dakota—this rooted him to the here and now, and that was probably more dangerous.

Elliot urged his horse forward and edged their mounts closer together as he caught up. Elliot pushed his hat farther down onto his head, water-blue eyes squinted in the low-angled sunlight. The older drover gave him a curt nod of greeting.

"So you hired the kid." It was a statement not a question.

"Yep."

"You know much about him?" Elliot inquired.

"Not a whole lot. But he seems to know his stuff and he was pretty desperate for a job." It was the same question anyone around here would ask—what did they know about him? But a body was a body when you needed to round up four hundred cows.

"He's been to prison," Elliot said.

"What?" Andy looked over at Harley, who rode next to Dakota. "How do you know that?"

"Just do." Elliot made a clicking sound with his mouth and the horses eased apart again. "Keep an eye on him, is all."

As Elliot moved farther away, Andy continued to eye the kid in question. He couldn't even grow a full mustache and he had a faintly naive look about him, like dirty jokes would spoil his innocence. Harley appeared to say something to Dakota and she laughed, the sound skipping along the breeze and melting into the rippling grass.

Either Elliot was lying or the Bible-carrying kid had the best poker face Andy had ever seen. Either way, this drive was about to get a whole lot more interesting.

AFTER A FEW hours of riding, the sun was shining warm and golden on Dakota's shoulders. The air was warmer now, but the wind was cold when it picked up. Autumn could be like that—bitingly cold in the morning and then unseasonably warm, all within a matter of hours. But they were in December and while it still looked like fall around these parts, the wind promised change. The land was a succession of rolling hills as they headed toward the mountains, and meandering lines of rocky creek beds spider-webbed into the cleavage of the hills. Cold mountain water babbled across stones, giving extra moisture for clusters of trees to dig down their roots and drink.

They reined in by a copse of fiery-hued trees to have something to eat and let the horses graze. When the wind picked up, the leaves swirled off the branches, circling and spinning as they sailed out over the grassland, leaving the trees just a little barer—just a little closer to naked.

It felt good to dismount and Dakota stretched her back, letting the tension in her muscles seep away. She loved riding. When she was on her own ranch, she preferred jobs like checking on the cattle or the condition of the fences because it meant she could ride all morning, face to the wind and heart soaring.

The men dismounted, as well. Dakota had been watching them as they rode. She'd spoken with a few. There was Harley, the innocent-looking kid who sparked her maternal side. She didn't know what it was about him, but she wanted to ruffle his hair. Then there was Elliot, who was silent but not altogether unfriendly. Carlos and Finn were both in their midtwenties and had flirted a bit, that is until Elliot put his horse between them and drove them off with that annoyed stare of his. Dave was goofy and joked around a lot, his humor bawdy but funny, but he knew his way around a horse.

And then there was Andy. Andy hadn't made much contact as they'd ridden. He'd kept back, surveying the land and possibly just keeping to himself. It was hard to tell. She'd expected him to talk to her somewhat, but he hadn't said a word. She wasn't disappointed about that; she was wary. Andy wasn't a man to be trusted, and she resented that he acted so honest and straight-shooting. A man who could hide his character was worse than one who wore it on his sleeve, and it looked like Andy had learned to hide a few things.

Or he'd reformed. Which was more likely?

Dakota unbuckled the saddlebag and pulled out the food she'd packed. There were two multigrain bagels filled with thick slabs of cream cheese, some dried fruit and an apple turnover.

"Are you ready for a rest?" Dakota asked softly, stroking Barney's neck. "You really are a sweetheart, you know."

The horse bent to take a mouthful of grass and she patted his shoulder. He wandered off a few paces, seeming to enjoy his temporary freedom.

Elliot, Dave, Finn and Carlos were sitting together on some rocks by a dried-up creek laughing at something—probably a joke told by Dave. He seemed to be an unending fount of raunchy humor, mostly centered on the women he'd dated, who seemed a questionable lot. Harley sat alone, a little ways off. He was opening a foil-wrapped sandwich and his gaze flickered up toward her as if he'd felt her curiosity. She gave him a cordial nod, which he returned then turned his attention to his food.

Andy sauntered in her direction and she was struck anew with those Granger good looks. He was tall, broad-shouldered, and he had the rolling gate of a man who knew how to ride.

"Hi." Andy paused a few feet from her then nodded toward a patch of shade a couple yards off. "Care to eat with me?"

No, she didn't want to eat with him, but avoiding the man wasn't going to be possible. She'd taken the job, and part of that job was dealing with the boss, so she silently followed his lead and they settled themselves on their jackets to eat. Dakota unwrapped a bagel, the scent of whole wheat making her stomach rumble.

"Nice speech earlier," Dakota said, taking a bite.

"That's a rehash of another speech I gave when I bought the dealership. That was a complicated time for worker morale."

It was strange, because she'd never really thought of Andy as a successful businessman before—more like an improperly rewarded fiend. But he did have a good sense when it came to getting people to work with him, and a team of drovers was probably the hardest group to win over. Not that he'd succeeded yet, but they'd stayed, which was more than she'd expected.

"So—" Dakota paused to swallow a bite "—you're doing well with the dealership, then."

"Yeah." He nodded. "I've built it up. When I bought it, it was barely breaking even, but after three years, it's making a steady profit. That doesn't come easily."

He'd made money, but that didn't mean he was liked—she knew that well enough. Sometimes the wealthiest men were the most hated because they'd climbed on the backs of the little guy to get where they were. She was curious what sort of boss Andy was when he was away from the town that knew him so well.

"How many employees stayed?" she asked.

"Most of them. A few were ticked off at the change of management style, and it didn't take too long to encourage them to move to something else." He took a bite of his sandwich and chewed thoughtfully then shot her a smile. "I'm good at it, you know."

Was he bragging now? It was hard to tell. Didn't he realize that he was announcing this to the woman who needed extra jobs to keep the family business afloat? In the distance a flock of birds lifted like a flapping sheet and then came back down in a fluttering billow.

"Good at what?" she asked curtly.

"Making money." He shrugged. So he was bragging. It was in bad taste and she shot him a flat look.

"What?" He frowned. "Hey, I know you all wanted

me to go to Billings and fail miserably. Sorry to disappoint." He was silent for a moment. "I wanted this
ranch. Well, my dad's part of it, at least."

Dakota's swallowed. "You always made it pretty
clear you didn't want this life."

"I had to talk myself out of it," he replied with
a shrug. "Haven't you ever wanted something you
could never have? I wasn't going to get it, and I didn't
feel like waiting around for the rejection. My brother
was the heir and I was the spare."

"So if Chet hadn't been interested—" She wiped
some crumbs from her jeans.

"Yeah, if I'd had a fighting chance at running this
place, I'd have done it." He nodded. "But you've got
to work with what you've got. That's life."

They were both silent for a couple of minutes as
they ate. Dakota polished off the bagel and moved
on to the dried apricots, sweet and tangy.

She and Andy had their desire to work the land
in common, as well as their status as second-born.
She'd always wanted to work her family's land, too.
What would she have done if Brody had shared the
same dream? Ever since they were kids, Brody had
wanted to join the army. He played soldier. She played
cowgirl. Knowing her brother's ambitions, her only
problem was trying to open her father's eyes to reality. But what if her reality was more like Andy's and
she loved the land that she'd never inherit?

But even then, she would have loved the land
enough to keep it from developers. This community meant something to her, and outsiders didn't

understand the heart of Hope. Maybe this was part of his talent—drawing in his employees so that they liked him against their better instincts.

"So why a car dealership?" she asked. There had to be plenty of other business opportunities around Billings. It was the largest city in Montana, after all.

"It seemed like a sound investment." He gave her a wry smile. "But no one dreams of spending fourteen hours a day on a car lot."

"So it was about the money for you?" she asked.

Andy popped the last bite of sandwich into his mouth and spoke past it. "Money? Uh-uh. I needed a life. So I built one."

So he'd settled, and in the process made a small fortune. When there were people following their hearts and just about losing their land, that seemed unfair. He might have built a life for himself, but it had come at a cost other people were forced to pay. Apparently karma had been sleeping on the job.

"What about you?" he asked. "Ever wanted to see what was out there in the big, wide world?"

"I want the ranch," she said. It was all she'd ever wanted. "And I'm not giving up on that."

"All right, then," he said, a small smile on his lips. "Do you think you'll get it?"

"You think I won't?" she shot back. "What do you know about it?"

He put up his hands. "Just asking."

She sighed. Picking fights with the man wasn't going to make this drive any easier, so she decided to answer. "I think I'll get it. Eventually."

Somehow. She was the one at home, wasn't she? She was the one working extra jobs, working the land, poring over ledgers in the evening…

"I hope you do," he said quietly. "Because if you don't, it'll be years wasted and, trust me—there will be resentment. You might think you'll be all open-minded and forgiving, but it feels different on the other side."

Andy turned back to his food and she mulled over his words. She was driven, focused on her dream for the future, but what if things didn't turn out the way she expected? What then? She couldn't see herself in any other role than this one—cowgirl, rancher. Would she have the strength to start fresh? That was a scary thought.

Angry voices cracked the stillness and Dakota's gaze shot toward the other drovers. Harley and Elliot were on their feet, glaring at each other.

"Say it again, kid…" Elliot's voice held a threat.

"You're a gutless wimp—" Harley didn't seem to be taking his opponent's size into the equation here. Elliot's expression was one of derision and he cracked his knuckles slowly, one by one, the popping sound carrying more clearly than their words. Harley quivered with raw rage, that baby face suddenly looking a whole lot meaner. The other men moved back, out of self-preservation or an instinct to let the males fight for status, Dakota had no idea, but things were about to get ugly.

"Getting tense over there," Andy said, his attention fixed on the men with a directness that belied his conversational tone.

"Are you going to step in?" It was less of a question, more of suggestion.

Andy's expression was guarded and his muscles tensed. He didn't answer her. This was where Andy was going to prove himself or fall short.

Harley was smaller than Elliot by quite a bit, thinner, shorter. He was downright suicidal to be taking on a man Elliot's size, in Dakota's humble opinion. Elliot was tougher, harder, older. Elliot didn't even see it coming when Harley threw a punch and caught Elliot in the jaw. The bigger man staggered back, shook it off, then stalked forward, a deadly look in his eye.

"That's all you've got?" Elliot challenged.

"Hey!" Andy roared, rising to his feet, and Dakota was momentarily stunned at the sheer size of him. Andy was a big man, six foot one with broad shoulders, and when he fixed that direct stare on someone it was downright intimidating.

Elliot slammed Harley in the gut, doubling him over, and Andy arrived at the scene in time to grab Harley by the collar and toss him effortlessly to the side. He rolled twice before landing on his backside. Andy stood solidly between Elliot and Harley.

"That's enough." Andy's voice was low but it carried. Dakota hurried to where Harley sat on the ground, staring at a spot between his knees. He was probably trying not to vomit after that blow to his belly. She put a hand on his arm and he jerked it away then spat. Ironically, Elliot was probably the worse for wear after that short scuffle, but given any more time, Harley would have been in very rough shape.

"That was dumb," she muttered. "He's a whole lot bigger than you, if you hadn't noticed."

Harley didn't answer.

Dakota shook her head and stood.

Andy was staring down Elliot, both men of similar height, but of the two of them, Andy was bulkier.

"Let it go!" Andy said, meeting Elliot's furious gaze. "I'm serious. Let it go."

"Or what?" Elliot growled. "You'll fire me? You can't. I work for your brother."

"Don't push me, Elliot." Andy's tone was menacing and Dakota glanced at the other men. They were looking away uncomfortably. This was going to affect their pecking order, she was sure. After a couple of beats Elliot muttered an oath and stepped back.

"What was that about?" Andy demanded, whirling around to face Harley. "You threw the first punch—I saw that much."

"Nothing."

"Elliot?" Andy demanded, shooting an icy glare toward the other man.

"Nothing!" he barked.

Dakota could see that was as far as Andy was going to get with the two men. They obviously knew each other, had a few resentments stewing and weren't about to open up about it to the likes of Andy. Still, Andy had risen to the occasion in a way she hadn't expected. Faced with the testy tempers of a couple of drovers, he'd matched them and backed them down. That took guts and a certain amount of confidence that left her grudgingly impressed. Somehow she'd expected the city convert to have lost some of his country edge, but she'd been wrong about that.

"All right." Andy raised his voice so everyone could hear. "I'm going to say this once and only once. Anyone who gets himself beaten up on this drive is going to have to ride like that. You break it, it's gonna hurt like hell on horseback. Now clean up. We're heading out in five."

Carlos, Finn and Dave looked at Andy with new respect, and Dakota watched as Harley and Elliot headed off in opposite directions. That left Dakota standing alone, the remnants of her lunch lying in the grass a couple of yards away. She brushed off her hands and eyed the men around her.

"Idiots," Andy muttered as he came past her, his strong arm brushing her shoulder. He'd earned something this morning—something that would last for the remainder of the drive—and she was glad that he had. Every cattle drive needed a clear leader and, for better or for worse, Andy was theirs.

She gathered up the last of her wrappers and the food she hadn't eaten, and headed out to where her horse was grazing a few yards off. Barney had completely ignored the human kerfuffle and she envied him that ability. It would be nice to be able to take his place in the open plains, melt into the wind and skim over the waving grassland, leaving her worries about the future far away.

"Dakota."

She turned to find Andy looking at her with a gentler look than she'd seen yet. He had Romeo by the reins and he adjusted his hat on his head with his free hand.

"Watch yourself, okay?"

What was he worried about, exactly? She'd grown up with guys just like this; she knew how to deal with them. She'd even dated Dwight, who'd turned out to be twice as bad as these guys when he'd had a few drinks in him. Andy had said he was no lost kitten, and neither was she. She'd worked her father's land when Andy had been shirking responsibility, and she'd worked shoulder to shoulder with rougher men than these.

Andy still didn't look settled, but he gave her a nod and put a boot into the stirrup. He swung himself up into the saddle and surveyed the group with a slow, cool gaze.

She mounted once more, feeling more secure on her horse's back, and she kicked him into motion. She could feel Andy's gaze drilling into the back of her as she passed him. When she looked back over her shoulder, he gave her a nod, flicking the brim of his hat. But his granite expression didn't change. Apparently he didn't find anything to joke about in the present circumstances, and that was something she could finally respect.

This drive would be so much easier if Andy Granger could just live up to expectations and fail.

It would also be a lot easier if he stopped being so blasted human.

Sympathizing with him hadn't been part of her plan, and it still wasn't. They'd never been friends, and she didn't need to be now; she was only here for the paycheck.

Chapter Four

That evening when Dakota dismounted, her legs ached from the long ride. She didn't normally ride for a full day like this unless she was doing a cattle drive. On her own land, she'd ride out to check on cattle in the nearer pastures, even escape for a morning of riding just for the pleasure, but the hard riding—the pushing forward and the not stopping, riding from sunup to sundown—happened once a year and her body had to get accustomed to the trail all over again.

They'd been riding west all day and for the last hour, the lowering sun had blinded her until it finally slipped behind the mountains in a final explosion of gold and crimson. She stretched her back, the movement feeling good on her cramped muscles. Daylight was gone and, while the sky still glowed orange at their position beside the foothills, dusk had arrived.

A fire was already roaring in a makeshift pit, some lawn chairs set around it in preparation for tired, cold cowhands. The camp was pitched beside a copse of creeping juniper and spruce trees that provided some shelter from the steady wind. The tang of sap and tree needles mingled with the mouthwatering aroma of corn bread and beefy chili that made her stomach growl, and Dakota watched as the others headed straight to the table laden with food.

"Hot cocoa?" Lydia asked with a friendly smile. She wore a knitted scarf around her neck and some fingerless gloves.

Dakota gratefully accepted a mug of frothy cocoa, two large marshmallows floating on top. She took a sip and licked her lips.

"Delicious," she said with a smile. "Thanks."

Lydia had fried sausages, canned peaches and three tubs of sour cream alongside the chili and corn bread. Within a matter of minutes, everyone was served heaping helpings of the feast.

When her own family did cattle drives, Dakota would look forward to this time of day when the work was done and they could settle around the crackling fire, talking and laughing. People said more after they'd eaten. There was something about that open sky, the pinprick of stars and the snap of a fire that made the consequences of words feel further away. Her grandfather's stories were always more interesting on the cattle drive than at any other time. He'd dug deeper out there, told the tales that were more honest and painted people as they really were. If she wanted to learn about her ancestors, the cattle drive was the place to do it.

But this was different. This was the Granger drive, and most of the people here were hired hands.

There would be no family stories told, and it only served to remind her that from here on out, they were going deeper into the wilderness, beyond the reach of roads and of rescue. The next night wouldn't be this comfortable and they'd be working hard, not just riding, very soon.

Andy stood to the side with his uncle, Bob, arms crossed over his chest. There was tension between them that she could see in the way they stood, arms crossed, a few feet apart, not looking directly at each other—they were family but Andy wasn't much more popular with his own kin than he was with the rest of Hope. Andy had made the Grangers look bad, and the Grangers cared about their collective reputation in these parts. They had a name to protect.

The other men were around the fire, dipping their corn bread into their bowls of chili and bringing it dripping to their mouths. Everyone was hungry. Her gaze moved toward Andy. He looked a lot like his brother out here with those broad shoulders and, despite the tension, his kind eyes. Funny that she'd notice Andy's eyes when she of all people shouldn't be fooled by them. Dwight had kind eyes, too, but you put a drop of whiskey into him and he got nasty right quick.

Dakota stirred the healthy dollop of sour cream into her spicy chili then took a bite. Food tasted better by firelight somehow. She glanced up as Harley sank into a lawn chair next to her, his plate balanced precariously on one hand.

"Hey," he said, taking a bite of corn bread.

She nodded to him and turned back to her own food. This was the time to fill up because after this, they'd only be able to eat what they carried and the fare went downhill quickly. The heat from the fire could reach them easily enough, and she enjoyed the way it warmed her shins first.

"So what's he like?" Harley asked past a bite of food.

"Who?" She glanced in Harley's direction again to find the kid's gaze directed toward Andy.

"Mr. Granger," he said.

"Andy?" She laughed softly. It was definitely strange to hear Andy referred to as mister, but then he probably was called "Mr." all the time back in Billings. It was only here in Hope that he'd never stop being plain old Andy. "You afraid he's going to fire you after that dustup with Elliot?"

She cast Harley an amused look.

"Will he?" Harley looked less than amused.

"I have no idea." That was the honest answer. Andy had promised anyone who caused trouble a pink slip upon returning, but then, Harley's job was over once they got back anyway, so for Harley that wouldn't make much of a difference. "I highly doubt he'll send you packing at this point. We need the bodies. You're only here for the drive, I thought."

"Yeah." Harley gulped back another bite of food. "But if there was work, I might offer to stay on."

There it was. Harley was hoping to be a little less temporary.

"What are you doing out here, anyway?" she

asked, dipping the heel of her corn bread into the last of the chili in her bowl.

Harley didn't answer right away and she thought that maybe he wouldn't, but after polishing off his last sausage, he turned toward her.

"You want to know?" he asked.

"Yeah."

Dakota eyed him with new curiosity as he told his side of things—the story of what had brought him to Montana to begin with. He was old-fashioned, she realized, with a streak of wounded honor. There wasn't a lot of place for that in the modern world, but if it could fit in anywhere, it would be a place like Montana, where a man's word was still supposed to mean something without a legal contract to back it up. There could be so much drama behind the shuttered faces of these cowboys, so many stories that no one would even guess at. He sounded older than he looked with that wispy mustache and those soulful eyes, and he seemed to notice her expression because he shot her a rueful smile.

"What?" he asked.

"How old are you?"

"Twenty-two."

She chuckled. Twenty-two wasn't exactly grizzled. She was just about thirty, but she could sympathize. She remembered feeling awfully grown up at twenty-two herself. She'd already ended a relationship to an abusive alcoholic.

"You're still pretty young for those old-fashioned

ideals," she retorted. She still had the urge to ruffle his hair...what could she say?

Harley didn't answer and he looked away. His jean jacket was pushed up his forearms to reveal what looked like a tattoo. It was crudely drawn, though, in the shape of a Celtic cross. Dakota tilted her head to the side to get a better look.

"What's that?" she asked.

Harley pulled his sleeve down, shielding his arm from view.

"Life experience," he replied dryly.

There was more to his story and she was willing to bet it was a whole lot more interesting than any of them had been giving him credit for. But he deserved a warning.

"Elliot's tougher than you might think," Dakota said quietly. "Don't go picking fights with him out here. We're miles from civilization and I'd hate to tempt his baser instincts."

"Noted," Harley said quietly.

Harley's gaze flickered in Elliot's direction and he nodded. At least he'd heard her warning, and she could only hope he'd take it.

Dakota glanced in Andy's direction and caught him watching her. How long had he been doing that? He had a plate in his hand now and he was chewing, his expression thoughtful. When she noticed him, he gave her a slight nod in acknowledgment and turned his attention to his food.

Andy seemed different out here, too. He looked more like the rancher, the boss, and less like the prodigal son. There was something about the expanse of grassy plains—the jagged drops and narrow crevices—and the rugged mountains that soared above them, closer now than ever. This cocktail of rugged wildness brought men and women down to their most elemental selves.

Stock markets and numbers in a bank account meant nothing out there, but a man's character meant a lot. Leadership and survival was based on an internal strength, not an external counter, and the farther they got from civilization, the clearer that difference became. There were some people she'd trust with her life out in the wilderness and others she'd never cross town lines with. And Andy...

His green eyes were fixed on her again and she met his gaze evenly. She didn't know exactly where he landed in her estimation of men and their character at this very moment, but he was standing stronger than she'd ever imagined he would.

"Come get more, everyone!" Lydia called from the table. "Eat it before it's cold!"

Dakota rose. She'd make good on that offer—this was her chance to eat before the real work started. A smart woman always took a second helping.

LATER THAT EVENING Andy sat beside the low-burning fire, orange coals glowing against the dark ground. Of the four tents pitched on the far side of the fire, one glowed from the light of a flashlight. Apparently, Harley was reading. The horses munched hay, the sound peaceful and soothing. Andy was taking the first watch and Bob would take the second. He could hear his uncle's snores already from the back of the van where he and Aunt Lydia were sleeping. They were far enough out that wolves and coyotes could be an issue if they didn't have a lookout.

Andy grabbed a log and tossed it onto the fire. The coals erupted in a shower of sparks then the dry bark caught the flame with a crackle.

Andy wasn't the last one awake. Dakota stood by Barney, giving him one last brush before bed, but Andy had a feeling she'd been putting off going to bed until the men were out of the way. She could hold her own, but these ranch hands weren't her family's employees, which would change the balance of power there. She was just another drover on this drive, albeit a prettier version than the others. Her hair hung long and loose down her back, the milky white of her hands vivid in the pale moonlight.

She's beautiful.

He'd always thought she was gorgeous, but she'd been the one woman solidly out of his league. Dakota wasn't just "a girl," she was smart, opinionated and way better than any of them deserved. When she'd turned him down for Dwight, it had stung—more than stung. But then he'd met Mackenzie and Mack had actually returned his feelings. That had been the most passionate summer of his youth, but he still hadn't been content. Maybe he'd have done the same thing to Dakota back then if she'd accepted him. He hadn't exactly been mature and he'd had a mighty high opinion of his own masculinity.

Dakota finished with the horse and turned, freezing for a moment when she saw him watching her. He inwardly winced. He'd made her uncomfortable—that hadn't been the plan. He looked back at the log that had started to burn in earnest and he could hear the crunch of her boots as she came closer. She sank into the chair next to him.

"You're on watch?" she asked quietly.

"The first one," he said. "You going to bed now?"

She shook her head. "Not yet."

He found himself pleased to hear that. He'd assumed that she'd turn in and he'd be left with his thoughts, but a few minutes' worth of company wasn't unwelcome.

Harley's flashlight went out and the camp was silent and dim except for the crackle of the fire.

"You're doing better than I thought," she said, shooting him a wry smile.

"You expected me to crash and burn so soon?" Andy chuckled softly. "Sorry to disappoint."

"I didn't say I was disappointed," she replied. "You did well with Harley and Elliot. That could have gotten ugly."

Andy leaned forward, holding his hands out to the fire. "It might get ugly yet. They won't talk, so whatever caused it is still simmering."

"Harley did."

Andy shot her a look of surprise. Harley had opened up? This was information he needed but he didn't want to chance being overheard. He stood and nodded in the direction of the edge of the camp where moonlight illuminated the rough, prairie grass. Dakota rose and they made their way from the trees and tents to where the open countryside spilled out before them, bathed in the silvery wash of moonlight.

A few black clouds scudded across the star-studded sky, leaving faint shadows on the land beneath. A coyote trotted silently across the grassland, a fresh catch in its mouth.

"So what's the deal?" Andy asked quietly.

"Elliot is involved with Harley's sister," she said. "Apparently she's pregnant and wanted to get married. Elliot didn't want to. I'm not sure what happened, exactly, but Harley is under the impression that his sister could do better and he came to Montana to try and bring her back home."

Andy rolled this new information over in his head. So Elliot was about to be a father... He and Chet both. Andy found himself mildly envious. It was an intimidating amount of responsibility to have a family to support, but it was the kind of challenge that Andy had always known he wanted one day. He couldn't help feeling a small pang of envy.

"Elliot said something earlier," Andy said after a moment. "Something about Harley having been in prison."

"He didn't mention that," she said. "But he did have a tattoo on his arm that looked...amateurish."

A prison tattoo? The thought still didn't sit right with him. But then, maybe that New Testament in his pocket was more about new starts than it was about his past. His decision to take the kid on may have been a hasty one. Still, Andy was pretty good with judging character, and Harley hadn't seemed elusive.

"He doesn't seem like the type," Andy said after a moment.

A frigid wind picked up and Dakota shivered.

"Come here," Andy said.

She looked at him distrustfully.

Andy rolled his eyes and took her by the shoulders, positioning her closer to him. He angled his body so that he blocked the worst of it, but he liked having her this near to him. He dropped his hands and they stood there, barely inches apart. He was her boss—nothing more.

Dakota's hair whipped up in the wind and she pulled it back, tilting her chin up as she did to meet his gaze. She only seemed to realize then how close they stood together and she stepped back, a cautious look on her face.

"I'm not trying anything," he said, his voice low. "It's cold. That's all."

He cared what she thought of him, because while he might not be her favorite man, her dislike of him was at least honest. If she was going to resent him, it might as well be for the truth, not something false. And he wasn't making a move on her. Tempted? Yes, but controlled. If he ever did make a move, she'd be absolutely clear about his intentions.

"I know." She didn't sound as convinced as he'd have liked.

"You still think I'm a womanizer, do you?" he asked with a low laugh. "It's not true, you know."

"I knew you, Andy." She shook her head. "Dwight used to tell me stories about you."

Dwight Petersen was the reason Andy had backed off and never asked Dakota out again. Friends didn't move in on each other's girls. But Dwight had changed over the years.

He remembered one trip back home when Dakota had knocked a can of soda off the counter and it had exploded open, splattering the kitchen floor and bottom cabinets. While Andy's first instinct had been to laugh at the way she'd jumped a foot in the air, Dwight had laid into her, calling her an idiot and growling about how she'd better clean it up. A few others had grabbed towels and lent a hand while Andy had pulled his buddy aside and told him straight that he'd better get it together because Dakota wouldn't put up with that garbage for long.

He'd been right. In a matter of weeks she'd broken off their engagement, and Andy had been relieved. Dakota deserved better than a man who didn't know a good woman when he had one. Thinking about Dwight's rage still left Andy uneasy, years later, and it made him wonder what, exactly, Dwight had told her about him.

"Back then, I might've been a bit of a womanizer, but that was then. A lot of things changed—including Dwight, might I add."

Dakota smiled wanly. "You're telling me that while Dwight turned into a drunk, you improved?"

He laughed softly. "I grew up, Dakota. We all do it eventually…except for Dwight, apparently. My last serious relationship lasted four years, and I almost married her. I've been single for the three years since. I don't think you can exactly call me a rake. Not anymore, at least. There's got to be a statute of limitations on that."

Surprise registered in those brown eyes and he felt a surge of satisfaction. At least he'd be able to blow apart one of her preconceptions.

"I'd heard you were engaged," she said.

"See?" He shot her a grin. "I'm not half as bad as you think."

Ida had been a wonderful woman. He could have been happy married to her, but there was something missing from their relationship, something he'd been looking for and never quite found. His brother had managed to find it with Mackenzie, but it was one of those intangible qualities that made all the difference in a relationship.

"You still managed to garner quite the reputation, you know," she noted.

"And you always managed to see right through me," he retorted. "You never liked me, Dakota. You didn't hide your feelings too well."

She frowned at that, cast him a sidelong look and then turned her attention to the rolling countryside.

"I didn't hate you."

"Didn't say hate," he said. "But you didn't much like me, either."

She shrugged in acceptance of that and he smiled

at the irony. He'd never bonded with a woman before over her general dislike of him, but there was a first for everything.

"The thing is…you never fell for my act."

"So you admit it was an act," she shot back.

"Sure." He shrugged. "Every guy has an act." What man wanted to advertise the things that hurt?

"Is this an act now?" She looked up at him, her clear gaze meeting his, and he dropped the urge to joke or flirt. She was serious and he sensed that she needed an honest answer from him. If they were going to work together, she needed to trust him.

"I've got nothing left to fake," he said quietly. "I'm the least popular guy in town, trying to hold things together for my brother. I'm just trying to get the job done. People will think what they think. Don't worry. I know where I stand with you."

"Which is where?" she asked, a small smile on her lips.

"Halfway at civil."

Color rose in her cheeks and she looked away again. "I should get to bed, Andy. It'll be a long day tomorrow."

"You should." He'd known she wouldn't stay out with him long, but it had been nice all the same. There was something about being alone with Dakota under the big Montana sky that woke a part of him that had been dormant for too long…a part that wanted to connect, talk, share. It was a dangerous temptation and parting ways was probably the wisest choice right now. This was temporary and he had no intention of complicating matters.

She took a few steps toward the tents then turned back, those dark eyes glittering in the moonlight. "I don't want to be friends, Andy."

"I know." He shot her a grin. "We aren't. We tolerate each other at best. Like always."

She laughed softly and he felt a surge of satisfaction at having made her laugh in spite of it all. She turned away again, heading toward her tent, and he returned his gaze to the rolling countryside.

The land spread out before him in a comforting expanse of nothing. The horizon, dark and distant, still tugged at him as it always had.

Dakota might have never liked him much, but he'd always grudgingly liked her. She was strong, smart and capable, and perhaps the proof of those qualities was in her instinctual distrust of him. While the other girls thought they might be the one to hook him, she'd never been inclined to try.

And now he was the one who'd ruined her family's land. She still wouldn't be inclined and somehow that made him like her all the more. She was the one woman he could trust to be completely honest with him. And perhaps she was the only woman who wanted absolutely nothing from him.

She didn't want to be friends. And neither did he. He wasn't a lukewarm kind of guy.

Chapter Five

The next day the tents, bedding and food were loaded onto the pack horses and the team set out amid the early morning mist, climbing steadily up the foothills. The land was rockier and craggier here, the scrub that erupted from gullies and lined streams now dry and scratching. Lydia and Bob had headed in the other direction. They'd be back in two days, but with the Grangers also left their last contact with civilization for the next couple of days. Out this far, their cell phones didn't even work.

Dakota settled into the rhythm in her saddle, but her mind was sifting through more than the upcoming work of rounding up the cattle. She was thinking about her conversation with Andy in the moonlight. She'd been completely honest when she'd told him she didn't want to be friends. She had a lot of reasons to resent him, but standing out there miles away from home and the pressures awaiting her there, she'd felt something unexpected…she'd *liked* him.

Attraction was something Dakota could deal with. Attraction was nothing more than a biochemical reaction, but liking someone went deeper. And, yes, Andy was definitely attractive. He had those Granger genes, after all—the wide shoulders, smoldering eyes and perfect swagger in his boots. That wasn't extraordinary, though. There were any number of good-looking cowboys; calendar companies made a fortune off them. But *liking* him…

She'd always sworn she'd never be pulled in by empty flattery and she knew Andy from their childhood onward, so she was supposed to know better than to fall for his charms. Andy had been a teenager full of flash with no substance. Then he'd matured into a grown man who'd sold them all out to the highest bidder. So standing with him in the moonlight, listening to him tell her that he wasn't the cad she took him for…

For a moment she'd thought he was making a move on her. She would have known how to deal with that. But his respectful reserve? Before this cattle drive, she'd known exactly what to think of Andy and exactly where to file him. Now she wasn't as sure, and she had a feeling that would irritate her family to no end. For them, Andy was the villain, the scoundrel who'd ruined their livelihood. They didn't want to see any other side of him, and she didn't blame them. She didn't particularly want to see this side of him, either.

The team continued their ride westward, the rugged mountains growing ever closer as the air grew crisper. There was something about those looming peaks that made her feel smaller than ever in the countryside. Nature was bigger than the pride of human beings. Birch and aspens were more common now and the leaves were blazing in oranges and yellows. It was the kind of exuberant display that made her heart soar, if it weren't for other things weighing it back down.

A few deer watched them warily from the tree line and an elk or two could be spotted out in the middle of the plains, antlers raised in proud display. Heads would lower to the ground to graze then shoot back up at the sound of hooves echoed against stone.

They splashed across several shallow streams, the water babbling along smooth rocks, allowing the horses a chance to stop and drink. And when they did, she'd catch Andy looking at her. He never came close, but he still watched her with a guarded look on his face. Then Barney would raise his head, water dripping from his muzzle, and plod onward, hooves hitting rocks with a clatter as a cold wind whisked through her hair. She shivered. Her fingers were cold now and the tip of her nose. She rubbed her hands against her thighs to warm them.

Dakota had decided early that morning to ride as far from Andy as possible. But the closer they got to the mountains, the rockier and more narrow their path became and they were all forced into closer proximity.

"I can hear the river," Harley said, pulling his horse next to hers as they plodded along.

Dakota could hear the rush of water, too, so much deeper and intense than the trickle of creeks. It was still distant, but they'd be there soon, and on the other side would be the cattle.

"The real work starts today," she said, shooting Harley a smile. "You ready?"

"Always."

She was looking forward to this—the actual rounding up of the cattle. This was where they had less time for talk and their attention would be monopolized by keeping the cattle together and moving in the right direction. From today on out, she'd no longer be "the girl" on the drive, but another hand on a very big job.

Andy rode ahead of the team and for the next few minutes she could feel the anticipation growing with the men around her. This was what they'd signed on for.

"So what's your story with him?" Harley asked, nodding in Andy's direction.

"There isn't one," she replied.

"You sat up with him last night."

Irritation replaced her previous good humor. She wasn't about to have her reputation bandied about in the Hope gossip mill, and the fact that she'd had a conversation with Andy Granger didn't make her available for anything more than talk.

"I spoke with our boss," she said icily. "Got a problem with that?"

A leafy twig from a nearby tree slapped her in the chest and she pushed it away irritably.

"Hey, not picking a fight here," he said, easing his

horse away. "It just looked like there was something more between you, that's all. Just curious."

So they'd been observed last night. The realization frustrated her. She'd thought the conversation had been private—the moment between the two of them. Realizing that it wasn't came as a rude awakening, because anything more than a professional discussion left her feeling like a sellout herself. If there was one thing Dakota believed in, it was loyalty to her family, and memories of her emotions last night left her feeling guilty.

Plus, she didn't want anyone to get the wrong idea about her and Andy. She wasn't along for the ride as the girlfriend, she was a hired hand. The difference mattered—one relied on a man's feelings for her, and the other relied on her own skill.

Her father deserved her loyalty, as did her brother fighting overseas. Andy Granger deserved nothing, and she needed to keep her position here straight in her own mind, as well as the other drovers'.

And yet she *had* liked him and definitely found him attractive in the way his direct green eyes met hers, pinning her to the spot without once touching her. If he had made contact, she would have pulled back, stomped off…but he hadn't. He'd just looked at her and shifted where he stood to keep the wind from hitting her so squarely, and somehow that act of protectiveness had kept her rooted to the spot.

Dakota kicked her horse into a faster pace, leaving Harley behind. Harley might have opened up to her about his sister, but that didn't mean she needed a confidant of her own. She had her situation well in hand.

Hell Bent River was close enough to see now as they crested a hill. It was an oxbow river meandering through the foothills. The banks farther upstream toward the mountains were lined by evergreen trees and a spattering of deciduous saplings glowing orange in the late-morning sunlight. Overhead, great, boiling clouds were moving in and, for a moment, the sunlight vanished and the trees turned from blazing orange to dull sienna. They sparked back into glory as the clouds pushed past, but the sky looked like rain wasn't too far off. That was the effect of the mountains, pushing the warm air upward until storms crashed down in a regular rhythm.

Across the river, before a stretch of forest, several acres of grassland spread out and a few cows were scattered across it, grazing lazily.

The sight of the cattle brought with it a flood of calm. Cattle had always done that for her. She wasn't sure what it was about bovine grazing that settled her in the deepest part of her soul.

"From what Chet said, the rest of the herd should be further on," Andy said.

Was he asking her input? She glanced at him and he raised his eyebrows expectantly.

"These are just a few stragglers, but we're close," she confirmed.

Andy didn't answer, but she knew he'd heard her. Whether he liked it or not, he needed her expertise out here. It wasn't bragging to note the obvious—

she was better at this part of the drive than he was. The cattle would be spread out as far as they could comfortably wander over a summer, and it was the drovers' job to spread out wide and start moving them in toward the center. The river would act as a natural corral the cows wouldn't cross without some significant persuasion. It was an ideal setup.

The other drovers had reined their horses in close by and Andy raised his voice.

"Carlos and Finn, you go north. Dave and Elliot, go south. Dakota and I are circling around back to the west, and Harley, you stay with the pack horses and start setting up camp. Come west once you're done. We're bringing them all back to this spot here, and then we'll camp for the night on the far side of the river. First thing tomorrow, we'll take them across the river and start for home." He glanced around at the men who stared back, faces immobile. "Stay safe, take time to think, and let's do this!"

Andy glanced at Dakota and she pushed her hat more firmly onto her head and shot him a grin. "Let's ride!"

Without any further prompting, the six of them kicked their horses into motion, came down the other side of the hill and toward the river. The work had officially started.

ROMEO STRETCHED OUT beneath Andy, lengthening his stride. The horse's hooves thundered beneath him, a rumble that moved up his thighs and into his stomach. The river was wider and deeper than the other streams they'd crossed and he could feel Romeo tense the closer they came to the water. Ahead of him, Elliot was the first to plunge into the river, the water coming up to the horse's stifle as he slowed, pushing against the lazy current. Elliot urged the horse forward with a shouted, "Hya!" Behind him, Carlos surged in.

Dakota had slowed, taking up the rear, and Andy glanced back, wondering if she were keeping her distance from the other drovers for a reason. Had someone been bothering her when he wasn't looking? Because he had been looking…watching, observing. Women could ride with men and do the job equally well, but not all men saw them as equals. He wouldn't have a woman mistreated on his drive. Especially not Dakota.

The pebbles rattled under Romeo's hooves as they approached the river, but Romeo balked and Andy could feel it in the horse's muscles.

"Let's go, Romeo," he muttered, giving him a kick to get him moving in the right direction. But the second the water hit the horse's fetlocks, he backed out again.

"Romeo, move it!" Andy ordered. "Hya!"

The other men were coming up out of the water on the other side and Elliot had already looked back, taking in the situation.

Andy grit his teeth in irritation. This wasn't the way he wanted the drovers to see him—inept in getting his horse across a river. Leadership counted, especially now.

Dakota came up beside him and Barney's big body moved right up next to Romeo.

"Let the horse do the thinking," Dakota said, her voice low.

"I would if—" Andy started, but Dakota's expression held an order. She knew horses better than he did—heck, better than anyone around these parts—so if she gave direction, he'd be wise to follow it.

"Loosen the reins," she commanded.

He did as she said, letting the reins go so that Romeo could choose his own way, and as Barney moved forward into the water, so did Romeo. They rode side by side, their knees pressed together, as the water rose up the horses' legs, splashing against their boots as they came to the middle of the river. Romeo stayed close to Barney, and Barney, being the more experienced horse, led the way. The solid muscles of the animals beneath them flexed as the horses pushed forward against the current, and soon enough, their footing grew more solid and they clambered up on the bank at the opposite side.

"Thanks," he said quietly.

"It never happened. You were waiting for me." She shot him a smile and eased Barney away.

The other drovers carried on without a backward glance, horses prancing forward as the water dripped off their sleek bodies. The grazing cows looked up in interest, trotting away as the horses approached.

She'd rescued his image back there. She could have taken the reins and led Romeo across, but she hadn't. She'd made it appear that they'd simply crossed the river together when, in reality, she'd been giving his inexperienced horse the support he needed, allowing Andy to keep face at the same time.

"That's why I recommended Patty," she said, shooting him a sidelong look.

"Point made." He grinned. "I still like Romeo."

She laughed. "You just hate taking your brother's advice."

Maybe he did. Chet had gotten it all, and there were times he wished his older brother would come to him for advice, to need something from him—anything—that would allow him to be the savior for once. But that had never happened. What did Chet need from him when he had everything already?

Except for this—Chet had needed someone to look out for the ranch when he couldn't be there. He'd needed this favor, and Andy didn't have it in him to turn his brother down. They had their own tangle of resentments, but at the end of the day, they were brothers.

"I've been away for too long," he admitted after a moment of silence. "I'm used to being the boss in my own world, not the stand-in for my brother's."

"Me, too." Her voice was almost too quiet to hear her, and he nudged Romeo closer, closing the gap between them. "I'm the hired hand here, but at home, I'm the boss's daughter. Trust me, I know the feeling."

"And here we both are, stepping down to help out the same guy."

"No, I'm stepping down because I need the money."

Those brown eyes caught his for a moment before she looked away again. "I don't have much choice."

"I had no way of knowing, Dakota."

"I know."

She seemed to blame him all the same. He heaved a sigh. She'd be rid of him soon enough, anyway.

"But even if you'd left well enough alone, I'd have done this for Chet," she said after a moment. "He'd do the same for us."

Would Chet do the same for Andy? He hadn't yet. Chet had held on to this land with a stranglehold, and he'd showed no inclination to loosen his grip—just like their father had. However, this was temporary, and it would all be over soon enough. Then Chet could take over again and Andy would go back to his own life.

"So are you saying that you helping me out back there...that was for Chet?" Andy asked with a wry smile. If it was for Chet, that was going to sting, but it might be better to know it up front.

Dakota didn't answer, but the color bloomed in her cheeks and she looked softer again. There was something about those pink cheeks that melted away his need to win this one.

"Seems to me that in spite of my mistakes—and you have to know that I'm sorry for what happened to your land—you might actually like me," he said. "You could have let me look like a fool. You could have led me across like a riding student, but you didn't."

She pushed her hat back and wiped a hand across

her brow. "Don't start rumors now, Andy. I care about the integrity of our team. That's it."

But her expression had eased and there was a sparkle in her eye. She was warming up to him, he could see that much. Whether it would last was another story.

They rode due west, side by side, the sun warming their backs as they went. Harley peeled off and dismounted, and when Andy glanced back, Harley was loosening the ties on one of the pack horses.

"Give it time," Andy chuckled. "I'll grow on you."

As they cantered across the field toward the distant tree line, Andy knew for a fact that Dakota would never be a woman to lean back on. She was no quiet support, she was a mouthy challenge, and he liked that even better. Besides, she'd come back to lend a hand, and that said more to him.

If he'd made fewer left turns in life, he'd have liked to end up with Dakota Mason. But there was no undoing his past and Dakota wasn't about to step down for the likes of him.

The horses opened their strides into a gallop and Andy loosened his hold on the reins. Let him run! He looked over in time to see Dakota bending low over Barney's shoulder, and the bigger horse thundered beside him. She was inching forward, and in response, Andy flicked Romeo's flank with the end of the reins.

So she wanted to race. He couldn't help the grin that came to his face. This feeling he had as they rode across the open field, his heart racing as their horses galloped—it was best to remember it was short-term.

The land, the ranch, the cowboy life—Chet had it all. Andy's life was in the city. And what was it that their dad used to say? *Timing has a lot to do with the outcome of a rain dance.*

He could have danced until his feet were raw, the ranch had never been an option. Andy had done what he'd needed to do, and he knew that looking back wasn't productive. But when he looked to the side, there was nothing better than a woman matching your stride, ponytail bouncing behind, body surfing the rhythm of the animal beneath her...

But the timing wasn't right for Dakota, either, and keeping his eyes forward was the best thing for him.

Chapter Six

Rounding up the cattle was a release, as if a spring had been snapped and everything holding Dakota back had suddenly flung away. This was the kind of work she loved—riding at full gallop across a field as she angled around a group of cattle. Then she'd pull up, head them off and heel her horse into motion again.

Barney knew this work, too—a reason why she'd chosen him. The horse loved this part as much as she did, and she could feel his joy as they raced across the land together, mane and hair blowing back in tangled knots that would take forever to brush out. But worth it. Oh, so worth it.

Andy worked about a hundred yards off. Romeo had been a good choice for this part of the job. He was young and wound up like an explosion about to happen. He could turn on a dime, and Andy held him in easy control. He held the reins close and tight, his knees gripping expertly, and when his gaze passed over her, he shot her a grin.

Andy could ride. It was odd to only be realizing his skill level now, and she found herself feeling grudging respect. She should have had a sense of what he could do, since they'd been on horseback for two days now, but this kind of riding was different than the slow plod toward the herd. This was daring—it took guts, and it took an instinctive trust of the animal beneath you.

"Surprised?" He laughed as he cut off the last of the escaping cows and reined in next to her.

"A bit," she admitted ruefully.

"We can't all be horse whisperers like you," he said, Romeo's hooves dancing beneath him. "But I can hold my own."

She had to admit he was absolutely right about that. He was holding his own quite admirably, and for a man who hadn't been honing his skills for the last decade, he obviously had natural talent. Had his family realized this? she wondered. Or had it gone unnoticed?

"Over there!" Dakota pointed toward some cows making a dash for the golden, blazing tree line. They exchanged a look and then heeled their horses into motion. The trees were like a carpet of autumn glory rolling up the mountainside. The farther up the mountain, the sparser the deciduous trees were, heartier evergreens taking over in the shallower, rocky soil.

The cattle had a lead on them and Dakota's heart sank as several cows disappeared into the foliage. Rounding up the cattle in an open space was a much easier task than winding after them through the trees.

"Blast it!" she heard Andy mutter, and she mirrored his sentiments.

"How many went in?" Dakota asked. "I counted three."

"Me, too," he confirmed, and he let out a shout, turning around a couple steers heading toward the tree line, as well.

"Let's go in on foot," Dakota said as they approached the trees. Riding in would be more difficult, and the cows would naturally run from them. But if they went in on foot, they could get closer and encourage the cows back into the open.

They both dismounted and went in a few yards apart to try to get around the sides of the cattle and get behind them. The trees were ablaze in golds and oranges, but once they went in, it was dimmer. The fragrant leaves under their feet crunched.

"There's one," Andy said, picking up a long switch as he angled around the other side of the steer. He swatted the steer's rump and it bawled out its annoyance but headed back in the right direction. Dakota took over as the cow came closer and spread her arms to encourage it to keep moving. It erupted into the open and she turned her attention to the next cow.

It took about ten minutes to get all three cows out of the trees and back into the field. When the last one shot back out into the open sunlight, she and Andy shared a grin.

"We work well together," Andy said.

"You're actually good at this," she laughed. She could remember Andy shirking the work the few times their ranches had worked together for harvest or calving.

"Why so shocked?"

"I always thought you went to the city because you didn't have what it took." She winced. "Sorry. Is that too blunt?"

He rolled his eyes. "What made you think that?"

"That spring when you helped us with calving. My dad had that awful stomach flu, remember? We went around tagging calves. You and I were put together, and you were all aloof and disinterested in the whole process. I remember that because you didn't tag one calf. I did it all. You were just along for the ride."

"You wanted to do the work," he replied with a small smile. "You were so eager and serious."

"I was not." Had she been? She'd been responsible. That was different. "You were lazy."

"I could do the work—better than most, might I add—but I wasn't about to get in your way. You kept plowing on ahead of me every time you spotted a calf."

Dakota thought back on that summer and maybe he had a point. She'd been pretty focused then. She'd been fifteen with precisely one interest—cattle. What did that make her, a cattle nerd?

"Besides, being capable with the work wasn't what my dad was looking for," he added.

"No?" Twigs snapped under their boots as they made their way to the tree line. "What did he want?"

"He wanted a team player," he said.

They emerged into the sunlight and Dakota went over to where Barney stood waiting and scooped up the reins.

"And you aren't a team player?" she asked over her shoulder before she swung up into her saddle. The cows were grazing again a few yards off and farther away still the whoops and shouts of the other drovers filtered across the distance toward them.

Andy mounted, as well, and pulled Romeo up beside her.

"Not really," he said with a glint in his eye. "I can go rogue from time to time."

Going rogue was an understatement. He'd sold his land and left town. If that was what he called going rogue, then she could well understand his father's reluctance to groom him to take over. Accumulating that kind of land took generations and a lot of money.

"Like with Mackenzie?" she queried. He paused, shot her a sharp look. She'd crossed a line with Mack, but she wasn't sure that she cared. She wanted to know.

"What about Mackenzie?" he asked.

"You cheated on her."

"Does everyone know about that?" he asked with a shake of his head. "I was seventeen. She and I had started up fast and hot, and I didn't know how to take that forward. What was I supposed to do, get a job and marry her? I wasn't mature enough to handle that kind of intensity in a relationship. I got scared and did something stupid."

"Hmm." She was silent for a moment. "Do you wish you'd been the one to marry her?"

Andy shot her a grin. "You're meddling, Dakota."

"You never come back for the holidays." She pressed on. "Talk around Hope is that you were in love with Mack and you can't bring yourself to see them together."

"That's crap." His tone was tired but not defensive. "I don't come back for Christmas because it reminds me of when my mom died when I was thirteen. When Dad was still around, I came home for the holidays because it still felt like Mom was here... in our memories. But when Dad died, there was no point. Christmas has never been the same since."

She'd remembered that his mother had died, but she hadn't tied that to Christmastime in her own mind. Obviously, Mrs. Granger's death hadn't impacted her own Christmas one bit back then, and for that she felt a wave of guilt. The Granger boys had lost their mother that year, and it hadn't even put a hitch in her stride.

Dakota cleared her throat. "I'm sorry. I didn't realize that."

"Yeah, well..." He shrugged.

"So what do you do for Christmas?"

"I get together with some friends, we have dinner out at a restaurant, open a bottle of wine at home."

She winced. "Not much for family."

"It passes the time," he said wryly. "And I know what you're going to say. That's not what Christmas is supposed to be. It isn't supposed to be endured.

But I'm not what a son is supposed to be, either—or a brother. So I do it my way. It's…easier."

They urged their horses into a trot and the cattle ahead of them started a slow move in the right direction. Dakota eased wide to keep a mother and calf moving, then edged back in toward Andy again.

"You and your mom were close?" she asked.

"Of course." He sighed. "And that was all Dad needed to solidify his view of me. Chet was his son, and I was Mom's son. My role in this family was set in stone long before I disappointed everyone."

Had he been pushed into the role of irresponsible younger brother? She'd never known Mr. Granger very well. He'd been quiet and stoic like most ranchers, but he hadn't seemed unfair or mean.

"What role?" she asked.

"I was supposed to work for my brother. I was supposed to do what Dad said, and when Chet took over, I was supposed to follow his orders."

"Ah." It was coming together for her. Andy had been expected to take his place as a support for Chet, and Andy had resented that. Perhaps that shouldn't surprise her—Andy and Chet had equally strong personalities.

"What do you mean, 'ah'?" he asked with a laugh. "Does that explain it all to you?"

"Yes."

Andy smiled wryly but didn't push the issue.

They rode in silence for a few minutes, her mind going over this new information. Andy was more broken than she'd realized. He'd covered well with his playful antics and disregard for rules, but there had been a lot more going on under the surface than she'd ever guessed.

"You were the opposite." Andy's voice broke into her thoughts. "I can analyze you, too, you know."

"You think so?"

"You weren't meant to inherit that ranch, either, but you knew Brody didn't want it, so instead of getting all disenchanted with the whole thing, you just got more persistent. You had something to prove and you wouldn't let the likes of me get in your way."

"The likes of you?"

"Am I wrong?" he countered.

No, he wasn't wrong. In fact, he'd nailed it, irritatingly enough. She'd been determined to prove herself worthy in her father's eyes, and maybe that had never stopped. She was still trying to get his approval, to show her ability. She was even taking on the financial responsibility to save up enough money for the down payment on the irrigation system. She could have left that one to her father. It was technically his ranch, after all.

"I'll take that silence for consent." Andy chuckled. "Don't worry. Your secrets are safe with me."

"What secrets?" How well exactly did he think that he knew her?

"That you're still scared you won't inherit that land," he said, his direct gaze meeting hers in a challenge. "That you're still scared you aren't quite good enough."

"Oh, I'm good enough," she retorted.

"I know it," he said. "But I'm not the one you're trying to convince, am I?"

Figuring him out was like a perplexing puzzle, but having him turn that same microscope onto her was mildly unsettling. She had more in common with him than she cared to own, but he was right. She was still trying to prove herself, and the only times she felt free of that burden was when she was out with the cattle, feeling the wind in her face. Out here, away from town, away from her father, away from all those pressures, she got to simply be.

And maybe that was something else she had in common with Andy Granger. Because out here he looked freer, too.

DAKOTA GOT QUIET after that and Andy wondered if he'd said too much. He hadn't meant to shut her down. It was nice to talk to her. Of all the drovers, she was the one he felt most comfortable with— maybe even too comfortable if he was talking this much. But they had personal history. She'd been his best friend's girlfriend. Heck, he'd expected her to become his best friend's wife. They'd been together long enough.

There was something about how she reacted to the mention of Dwight, though. She shut down, froze over. It'd been several years since their split, and that kind of reaction seemed a little extreme for a couple that didn't work out. He wondered what happened there—what Dwight hadn't told him.

When Dwight and Dakota broke up, they'd been

the focus of the Hope rumor mill for months. Andy had talked to Dwight a little bit when he'd come back for Thanksgiving long weekend from school, but they hadn't had much to say to each other anymore. Dwight had stayed around town and hadn't gone to college. Andy had gone to school and had a head full of business and economics.

Truth be told, Andy had thought himself better than Dwight at that point in his life. He wasn't proud of that now, but youthful arrogance had no bounds. Add a few years and a bit of life experience, and a man knew that four years of college didn't add up to anything much when it came to human value, but college freshmen weren't always clear on that, and his glossy vision of his own future had been shinier than anything else right then. So he didn't blame Dwight for not opening up too much. Now that Andy had experienced a broken engagement of his own, he knew exactly how much pain his buddy had been in. His empathy was several years too late to be much use to the friendship, though.

Regardless, Dwight had clammed up and not said much other than it hadn't worked out and Dakota had called it off. Dwight had moved back in with his mom for a bit to lick his wounds, and Andy had given him an awkward pat on the back and said something banal about there being more fish in the sea.

Again, not Andy's proudest moment.

He wished now that he'd been a better listener, because from what he could tell, Dwight had sunk into depression. The last he'd heard from him, Dwight had been talking about some sports bet he'd lost on. Andy had felt bad for him, but hadn't lent him any money to cover it. By then they'd grown apart. They had different interests, different goals, and the only things they had in common were high school memories that felt further away than ever.

One of those shared high school memories was Dakota—a memory that was in the flesh on this cattle drive—the girl who'd chosen Dwight over him.

The cattle were moving steadily toward the river now and the other drovers were closing in. This made the job harder as four hundred cows got pressed ever closer together. It was organized chaos at best. Andy was tiring—this pace was a grueling one to keep up.

Andy whooped, pushing the cattle farther in, and the thunder of hooves and echo of bawling cattle thrummed through him. Where was Dakota? She was around here somewhere—close by, surely, since they'd been riding together only a couple of minutes ago. He looked around then whooped again, heading off a cow that tried to escape.

"Hya!" he shouted. "Get on!"

The cow zagged back into the herd, and Andy scanned the mad, writhing team of cattle. It was then that he saw her—directly in the path of steer about to make a stand. Its hooves were spread, head down, nostrils flared—signs of an angry animal. Dakota's horse seemed to sense a personal assault because Barney reared up, pawing the air and, for a split second, Andy's heart stopped in his chest. But Dakota stayed seated, perfectly in control of her body, and he let out a pent-up breath of relief. Andy was impressed watching her ride out Barney's rearing, but as the horse came down, the steer thundered toward them.

Andy kicked Romeo into motion, intending to head off the steer, but before he could intercept, Barney lowered his shoulder and heaved backward, tossing Dakota clean out of the saddle as if she were a doll. She landed on the ground with a jarring thud.

Andy arrived at that moment and inserted himself between Dakota and the steer, shooting out a hand.

"Dakota!" he shouted.

She pushed herself to her feet and reached up, grabbing him by the forearm, allowing him to pull her up neatly behind him into the saddle just as the steer charged around them again.

"Thanks!" she panted as he heaved a sigh of relief.

"No problem." He looked around for Barney and saw the big black horse not far away. He headed in his direction. "Are you okay?"

"It hurt, but I'll survive." Her voice was breathy and he could tell she was in pain. It felt strangely good to have her behind him—so close that he could feel the pounding of her heart against his back. Thank goodness he'd been close enough to get to her...but still, he had a feeling she hadn't exactly been in distress. She dealt with horses and cattle on a daily basis.

When they got to Barney, she swung down and grabbed his reins. She rubbed a hip with one hand and scowled into the horse's face.

"Not nice, Barney," she remonstrated, and Andy could have sworn he saw guilt in Barney's expression. Then she put a foot into the stirrup, grabbed the horn of the saddle and swung herself up.

"You sure you're okay?" he asked.

"You act like I've never been thrown before." Her expression was incredulous, and Andy shook his head and laughed.

"Just checking. Let's work, then."

It was quite possible she was tougher than he was, even with their difference in size. She was petite and slender, while he was tall and bulky, but she could probably take more of a beating from a horse than he could and still stand afterward.

He wouldn't be able to do this job without her, he realized. He didn't like that fact. He'd much rather know that he could do this with his hand tied behind his back, but he knew better than that. Dakota had been quietly, unobtrusively, supporting him on this drive, and if he didn't have her here, he'd likely have lost the drovers' respect by now.

She was helping him succeed...but why? Why would she do this for him when he was Enemy Number One in her family? Why put herself out for him at all? He glanced back over his shoulder. She didn't notice his scrutiny and he was struck anew by her beauty. Sitting there on the big black stallion's back, hair blowing out behind her in the brisk wind, her cheeks reddened from exertion and weather, he found himself feeling something he hadn't felt since he was a teenager.

She should have chosen me. When she'd had the choice between him and Dwight, Dwight had been the lucky dog who'd got to spend his weekends with Dakota Mason. Andy had always cherished a little pang of jealousy because of that. He'd tried to put it to bed, especially after Dwight had asked her to marry him, but it was still there.

But this was a decade later. They'd all grown up, changed, started lives of their own… It was time to stop envying Dwight the time he'd had with her, because here Andy was with Dakota on a cattle drive, and if he really wanted to do something about it, he could.

Or could he?

Life was cruel, because while he sat here staring at Dakota Mason, realizing just how amazing she was, there were too many reasons to hold back. Her family hated him. She was as tied to the land as Chet was, and Andy was heading out just as soon as he could manage it. He was a grown man, and this was not a possibility.

He'd best keep telling himself that, so he didn't do something stupid.

Chapter Seven

Rounding up the cattle kept everyone busy for the rest of the day. Whoops and shouts followed the wind across the plains as they rode, herding the cattle from the farthest reaches they'd wandered. The drovers came at the cattle from all sides, driving them steadily into a central area. Cattle could be ornery, and they bawled out their frustration at being herded, the air filled with the shouting voices of cattle and men alike.

Romeo had the energy and quick responses as Andy wheeled him around to cut off a bolting heifer—a grudging point in his favor for his choice of mount. As for Barney, he was an experienced horse and he knew what Dakota wanted from him before she even had to tug the reins. She and Andy worked well together, teaming up to cut off the running cows and herd them in the right direction.

Andy seemed to relax into the job, and if she didn't know about his life in Billings, she would have thought he was a lifelong rancher. It was in his blood—the Grangers had been in these parts for more generations than even the Masons had—and watching him work showed her a side to him she'd never seen.

Not only was he was good at this, but there was something about the look in his eye when his lips tightened to let out a sharp whistle from between his teeth that sped up her heart just a little bit. It was his instinctive ability, his intensity, and the grin of victory when he succeeded in rounding up the escaping cattle that gave her pause. Andy wasn't the spoiled city boy she'd cast him as—there was more to him than she'd given credit for.

Her father would hate this, and at the thought of her father, a wave of guilt crashed down over her. She owed her loyalty to her father, not Andy.

Four hundred head of cattle were a big job for six drovers, and they worked steadily through the day. There was no time to stop for breaks, and by the time they'd brought the cattle together into the field by Hell Bent River, the sun was setting and Harley had a fire roaring.

As Dakota rubbed down her horse, the smell of hot biscuits and stew made her stomach rumble. It looked like the kid knew how to cook over a fire, which was a welcome discovery. There was nothing worse than finishing up a day of hard work only to find that your dinner consisted of burned beans and crunchy rice. She'd been there, and it could inspire plenty of rage in the hungry drovers.

Now, with the workday over, Dakota was giving Barney a much deserved grooming. As she pulled the curry comb over his black shoulder, Barney's muscles trembled with pleasure.

"Hey…" With the word came a cloud of booze-smelling breath, and Dakota startled, memories of Dwight flooding back like a punch in the gut. How many times had Dwight approached her just like that? Her stomach curdled and she looked irritably toward Elliot, a flask in one hand and an intent, glittery look in his eye.

"I saw you working with Andy today…" Bitterness tinged his tone. "He seems to like you a lot."

The words were only slightly slurred. He was intoxicated but not diminished—a dangerous combination she was only too familiar with. She looked around. Where was Andy? She could see him across the camp, his back to them. He was talking with a couple of other drovers, gesturing about something. Her gaze whipped back to the man in front of her.

"You aren't supposed to be drinking, Elliot," she said, stepping around the front of the horse so she could move farther away.

"Just a nip." Elliot laughed quietly. "You gonna rat me out?"

She wouldn't need to, and she shot the drover an annoyed look as he came closer. "Elliot, I'm busy. Go groom your horse."

Elliot fell silent for a moment and she pretended to focus on Barney, but her heart was hammering in her chest. Dwight had been like this, and she'd always thought she could talk him out of it, but she'd been wrong. It never ended without bruises. The only thing she wanted right now was to put some distance between them, and she moved around the other side of the horse. Only as she moved out of sight of the other drovers did she realize what she'd done, and her stomach curdled.

Stupid!

Elliot followed her, closing the distance quicker than he seemed capable of, ducking away from the snap of Barney's teeth. She wished Barney had managed to make contact, but Elliot was clear now, and coming closer.

"I think I know why Andy hired you," Elliot said, a slow smile spreading over his face.

"Because I'm qualified," she snapped. "Now, leave me alone."

"Want a drink?" He nudged the flask toward her.

"No." She took another step back, but he quickly closed the gap between them. "Elliot, leave me alone."

He reached out, presumably to touch her, but he missed, a grimy hand fumbling against the side of her face. Dakota pulled back in disgust and his hand fell to the front of her jacket. Whether his groping was intentional or not, her insides roiled.

"Elliot, get your hands off me!" she snapped. "And if you don't want—"

A heavy hand fell on Elliot's shoulder and Dakota looked up in wild relief. Elliot stumbled around to see Andy glowering down on him. Andy's normally relaxed expression had transformed to one of barely concealed rage. His hand tightened on Elliot's shoulder and he hauled him away from Dakota.

"Touch her again, and you deal with me personally," Andy growled. He snatched the flask from Elliot's fumbling grip and upended it, pouring the contents directly into the scruffy grass. "Rules say no booze. Chet will be hearing about this."

Andy shoved him toward the rest of group, now getting their servings of hot stew and biscuits. "And eat something!" he barked after the drover. "Harley, get Elliot some coffee!"

Dakota swallowed the bile rising in her throat. Elliot had scared her more than she'd wanted to admit. Sober, she could deal with him, but drunk—the booze was an impenetrable wall between the drover and his better instincts. She knew what that was like.

"Are you okay?" Andy's tone was still gruff but his eyes were gentle.

"I'm fine." She sucked in a wavering breath.

"Okay…" He clenched his jaw then slid a hand around her waist, tugging her gently toward him. She could have pulled back but she realized that she didn't want to and she followed his nudge toward him, allowing him to pull her against him. His heart beat loud and strong against her ear and she rested her face against his chest, gathering her senses once more.

"Next time, yell." His voice rumbled low in his chest.

She nodded then pulled back. "Deal."

"Come on." He let go of her and led the way toward the fire where the other drovers were already eating. Elliot sat to one side looking sullen, a bowl of stew untouched in his lap.

"Okay, men," Andy said, raising his voice louder than necessary. He glared around the fire. "I'll say it once, and after that, I'll stop being so professional and deal with you man to man. We have a lady riding with us. She's fast, strong and a heck of a drover, and I expect her to be treated like everyone else. Are we clear on that?"

The drovers stopped chewing and looked first at Andy, then at Dakota, then around at each other. They exchanged confused looks.

"Got it, boss," Harley said with a nod. The others echoed him.

"Mind if I ask," Carlos said. "Did something happen…?"

They cared, she could see that much. Elliot was drunk, but sober he was the one chasing off the others. She didn't want to be treated like "the girl," but she had to admit Andy's help hadn't come a moment too soon.

"I'm fine!" Dakota snapped. She was irritated, and not because the drovers cared about her safety, but because she shouldn't have to worry about her safety out here. They should all be equals, doing a job they were all good at. And while Elliot had scared her, she was even more annoyed she hadn't kept her head about her. She'd slipped out of sight—retreated. She was even angrier still that she'd been in that position to begin with. If she'd been with her father's

men, no one would have dared to try that, but she'd
been forced down in the ranks because of Andy's
idiocy when he'd sold his land. She wasn't the boss's
daughter, she was a regular hired hand who needed
the job for a little extra cash. She'd most certainly
fallen in the world, and it was entirely Andy's fault.

She headed toward the pot of stew and pulled off
the lid. Would she have been strong enough to fight
off a man Elliot's size who was already numbed by
alcohol? She'd have given it her best shot, but she
honestly didn't know. She hadn't been able to fight
off Dwight, but she'd also learned a few moves since
then... Brody had made sure of it.

She glanced back at the fire. The men looked uncomfortable and Andy barked at Elliot to eat up and
bed down. Elliot ducked his head and did as he was
told. Andy, by all appearances, wasn't going to let
go of this one easily.

Dakota scooped up a healthy portion of beef stew
from the cast-iron pot, reached for a couple of biscuits from the lopsided pile and, as she did so, noticed that her hand was shaking. She pulled her fist
hard against her side to still the trembling.

No man would make her shake. No man would
make her tremble. If she could kick a cow into sub-
mission, she'd do the same with some drunken drover
if need be, and she'd aim for his most vulnerable bits.

All the same, being the boss's daughter was a
whole lot more helpful in these situations than she'd
been willing to admit. She'd lost more than water
rights and an ability to make a decent profit. She'd

lost the status that protected her. Standing out here in the wilderness, surrounded by the soft lowing of cattle and the whistle of the cold, December wind, she'd never felt so vulnerable.

ANDY TRIED NOT to watch Dakota while she dished herself some stew. The air was cold and her breath came out in a cloud. She didn't want to be mollycoddled—he could tell that much. As he turned back to his own food, he could hear the distant howl of wolves from the direction of the trees. That sound was enough to put up his hackles. They'd stay clear of the fire, and they were easy enough to chase off on horseback, but if a pack got a calf separated...or, God forbid, a drover...

"Who is first on patrol tonight?" Harley asked, wiping the inside of his bowl with a piece of biscuit.

"I am," Dakota said.

Andy glanced up as Dakota joined them, sinking to the ground by the fire to start eating.

"I could take over for her," Harley suggested, and Andy was inclined to agree, if it weren't for the baleful glare Dakota shot in Harley's direction.

"Why, exactly?" she demanded.

"If it—" Harley blushed red. "I mean, it might help—"

"You think you're a better shot than I am?" she retorted. "I can ride better and I can shoot better. I'll be fine, trust me."

Was that an indirect threat he heard between the lines there? A warning for Elliot?

"There are wolves out tonight," Andy said. "We'll have two on patrol at all times. So Dakota is first, and I'll take the first patrol with her. At midnight, Dave and Finn, then at three, Harley and Elliot, and if Elliot can't get up, I'll patrol again with Harley."

Andy didn't want to let anyone else patrol with her. It wasn't only his protective instinct where she was concerned, though. He wanted some time with her—a chance to talk—and he was looking forward to that more than he probably should.

He wouldn't get much sleep, but that was the burden of leadership. Elliot wasn't carrying his fair share of the load, and if Andy had his way, he'd be fired at the end of this, but they needed him until they got back. He hadn't liked the way Elliot had been stalking Dakota. It gave him the creeps and ticked him off at the same time. There had been more to that encounter—Andy just couldn't put his finger on it. Anyway, Andy would put in some serious effort to waking Elliot come three. It wasn't like he'd let the man sleep like a princess.

The sky was cloudy, no moon or stars to illumine their position on the plains, only firelight flickering orange and crackling with warmth. Moisture hung in the air as a promise of rain, and if the temperature dropped, snow. It would be a cold night.

The rest of the drovers turned in shortly after that. When a man had to get up in the middle of the night to patrol, every minute of shut-eye was precious. Andy saddled up and Dakota wasn't far behind. He handed her a shotgun, then slung his own across his back.

"You said you can shoot, right?" he said.

"You still doubting me at this point?" she asked with a half smile.

"I'm just making sure," he retorted. "I'd rather not get shot tonight."

Dakota rolled her eyes—the only response he'd get—and kicked her horse into motion. Andy chuckled to himself and heeled Romeo after her, heading south along the riverbank.

The cows were mostly lying down, slowly chewing their cud. They looked up as Andy and Dakota rode slowly past, the stillness of the night interrupted by the distant, bone-chilling howls. Out here, they weren't top of the food chain.

"I'm sorry about Elliot today," Andy said. "I'll deal with him."

"It was the booze," she said.

"Even so, I'll deal with him." That was a promise. Even if Dakota would rather have him leave it alone, he'd still deal with Elliot for the simple reason that he'd scared her—he'd seen the stricken look on her face—and Dakota didn't scare easily. He had no idea what Elliot had said to inspire it, but he'd make the drover pay one way or another.

They rode in silence for a few more minutes and Andy glanced in her direction a couple of times, wondering what she was thinking about. Her expression conflicted.

"You okay?" he asked.

She glanced toward him then nodded. "Fine."

"You don't look all that fine." He glanced back toward the camp. "I'll keep an eye out for you from here on out." Not that he wasn't already, but he didn't exactly want to announce that.

"I don't need babysitting."

"It isn't babysitting. It's the decent thing to do," he said. "Besides, you've helped me out of a couple scrapes already on this drive. I figure it'll make us even."

She gave him a wan smile—acceptance of the terms, he imagined. Riding with her in the moonlight reminded him of all those feelings he used to harbor for her—the longing to show her he was better than she thought, and the jealousy for the buddy who got a chance with her.

"Do you still see Dwight around?" Andy asked after a moment.

"No." She laughed suddenly, the sound low and bitter. "I keep clear of him."

There was something in her voice that gave him pause and he frowned, nudging his horse closer to hers. "I know he was kind of a jerk toward the end—"

"Did you know about that?" she interrupted.

Was there more to this than a simple breakup? Or maybe Dwight had really broken her heart—it was a cancelled wedding, after all. He'd been able to sympathize with Dwight over the ended engagement, but she'd have had an equal share of that heartbreak.

"He seemed to take you for granted a lot," Andy said. "At least, that's the way it looked to me."

"Take me for granted…" She was silent for a moment. "Yeah, I guess so, but that wasn't the biggest issue. He beat me up."

Andy felt the words hit him like ice and he whipped around and stared at her in disbelief. "He *what*?"

"He beat me up," she repeated, and it was like her words echoed in his head. "Every time he got drunk and I was dumb enough to go over to his place when he called, he'd go into some violent rage and smack me around."

The very thought of Dwight raising a hand to her was almost unbelievable, but then, how well had he actually known Dwight later on? Hot rage welled up inside him, overtaking the shock and giving him the urge to go find the man and pound on him.

"I didn't know that," he growled. "If I had—"

"You'd have what?" she countered coldly. "Told him to smarten up? Shaken your finger at him?"

Her words were sharp but her eyes misted a little as she said them. He could tell that her anger covered over a lot of pain—pain that had probably been reawakened by Elliot.

"I'd have hit him back for you," he retorted. "And I'd have made sure he didn't get up too easily, either."

An image arose in his mind of his fist connecting solidly with Dwight's grinning face. What kind of man raised his hand to a woman? Andy rifled through his mind, looking for clues he should have seen. How could his best friend have been beating on his girlfriend, and Andy didn't know?

"You should have told me," he said suddenly.

"You were away at college," she said. "I did one better and I told my brother."

Brody—yeah, that had been a good call on her part. Brody was now overseas with the army, but he'd always been about as soft as a tank. If she'd told her brother, he'd have taken care of it, although Andy would've enjoyed being part of the solution.

"How long was that going on?" Andy asked.

"He hit me on three different occasions," she replied. "I should have dumped him the first time, but what can I say? I wasn't smart enough back then. But the third time, I threw his ring back in his face and went home. Brody saw the black eye and hit the roof."

And no one had told him about this. Either no one knew and it was all hushed up, or he'd been too distanced from everything back home to even notice. Dakota had been right about one thing—he'd been pretty intent on getting out of town for good back then. If he'd been there, though—

"And that's why Elliot scared you so badly," he concluded, everything falling together in his mind. "He was drunk and wouldn't leave you alone, a whole lot like Dwight."

"A whole lot like Dwight." Her words were low.

They rode in silence for a few minutes, Andy's mind going over her words like a broken record. Dwight had been his buddy ever since junior high. They'd hung out on weekends and collaborated on science projects. Dwight had thrown Andy a birthday party just before he'd left for college, and Dakota had been there for once. She normally didn't have much to do with Dwight's friends. Everything had seemed fine—Dwight was head over heels for Dakota, and Dwight's parents treated Dakota like a daughter. They'd both been eighteen, and Andy was off to college in the city.

Then in the space of a few years, that fun-loving guy, the loyal buddy, had turned into a violent lout. If she'd just taken a chance on him instead, all those years ago when she'd had the choice between him and Dwight... But that was in the past. If wishes were horses—how did that saying go?

"Did you see any signs of it before?" Andy asked. What he was really asking was if there was anything he could have done while he was still around.

"He had a temper," she replied with a shrug. "But I'd never dreamed he'd lift a hand to me. That's why it took me three incidents to finally leave. It felt so surreal, so impossible."

Seeing Dakota flinch like that when Elliot had bothered her stuck in his head. She'd reacted in fear, and the thought of Dwight hurting her, scaring her, traumatizing her like that, stabbed him. He'd seen Dakota's body language when she'd backed away and Elliot had moved in like a predator. That was when Andy went to investigate. He'd taken care of it, but no one had been there to protect her from Dwight.

He was my friend.

He felt a pang of guilt at that little fact, although Dwight wouldn't count as a friend anymore. And

Andy couldn't do too much about what had already happened. That was the most frustrating part about this—hearing about what Dwight had done and not being able to fix it himself... Because given a chance—

The howl of the wolves seemed to be moving farther away and Andy paused to listen to the lonesome sound. The cattle shifted uncomfortably—their instinct would warn them of the danger. The horses' hooves plodded evenly as they came along the edge of the herd. A few yards away, something moved—almost flopped. It was hard to see the in the darkness, and Andy pulled out a flashlight, shining it toward the spot.

A half-grown calf lay next to its mother. It struggled to stand again, but couldn't. This was a much younger calf than most of the others, and Andy reined in his horse.

"Dakota, do you see that?" Andy asked. He dismounted and gave the horse a pat before heading in the direction of the calf. A couple of cows rose and ambled a few paces off, but the mother stayed immobile, big liquid eyes regarding him.

She knew he was here to help, and he looked back to see Dakota coming the way he had, a few paces behind him. Andy squatted next to the calf and he could see the problem. It had gotten tangled up in a piece of twine that had bound its back legs together in a painful snarl.

"Poor thing," Dakota said as she arrived. "Use your knife. I'll hold its head."

She crouched next to him and took the calf's head in her hands, crooning softly to it about how everything would be just fine in a minute. Andy pulled out his pocketknife and sawed at the twine until it snapped, freeing the calf from its awkward position. It immediately bounded to its feet.

"There." Dakota released the calf and fell back as it lunged out of her grip.

Andy held out his hand and she put hers in his calloused grip. He boosted her to her feet. But once she was up, he didn't let go, and she didn't pull free, either. Maybe he was more comforting than he thought. She paused, her dark eyes glittering in the moonlight, and he flicked off the flashlight, drinking her in. What had she been going through while he'd been away? And why hadn't she given him that chance? Why hadn't he tried a little harder to get her attention? He'd been acting like his older brother, stepping back when the woman chose another guy, but Dwight had been a bad choice—worse than he'd ever realized.

They walked together around the cows and back toward the horses, and he kept her hand in his own tight grip. A cold wind whipped across the plain, the whistle mingling with the river's rush. He felt her shiver and tugged her closer against his shoulder.

She complied. When he turned to face her, she didn't pull back. The wind ruffled her hair around her face and as she looked up at him he found himself thinking all sorts of things he knew were out of bounds. But there was something about those dewy eyes and her parted lips… He took her face in his hands, running his thumbs over her wind-reddened cheeks.

"I asked you out," he said softly.

"What are you talking about?"

"Back when you started dating Dwight, I asked you out," he said. "And I'd been serious, you know. It wasn't me flirting or just trying my luck. I'd had to work up my courage to ask you."

"I'd already started dating Dwight," she said, shaking her head. "I wasn't that kind of girl."

No, she hadn't been. Dakota had been quality, the kind of woman who was loyal and principled. Right and wrong mattered to her, and she stood by her convictions. She'd most definitely not been the two-timing sort.

"I wish you'd have made an exception," he said. "Because I'd never have hurt you."

She pulled back and he released her. Had he offended her? It was true, though.

"I didn't need rescuing, Andy."

Dakota had never been the kind of girl who'd admit to needing rescuing. She'd had it all under control—at least the parts she let the rest of them see. She knew what she wanted and she went for it. But back then she'd been faced with a decision on who to let into her life, and she'd made the wrong choice, in his humble opinion. By the time she'd figured that out, he'd been long gone, building a life in the city.

"Just tell me I would've been a better choice." He

caught her eye and held it. She pulled in a breath, and he stepped closer. "I'd be happy with that."

She put her hands to his chest. She only came up to his shoulder, but when she tipped her chin back to look him in the face, his lips hovered over hers. Their mingled breath was a wisp of cloud in the cold night air. She didn't answer him and, instead of questioning it further, he did what he'd been longing to do for several days now and lowered his lips onto hers. She didn't pull back. He kissed her gently, chastely, then stopped, looking into her face.

"You were the better choice," she said softly, a smile coming to her lips.

"That's what I'm talking about," he said with a low laugh, and he gathered her up into his arms. This time when his lips came down onto hers, she leaned into his kiss and her eyes fluttered shut.

She felt warm and small in his embrace, and as she strained upward toward his kiss, he felt a wave of protective longing. This was what he wanted—this impossible moment right here. He wanted wind and space, cattle and horses, and he wanted this woman in his arms. He wanted her so badly that his whole body ached with it.

When she pulled back, he reluctantly released her and his arms feeling cold and empty, the dampness of her lips still warm on his mouth.

"Wow…" she breathed.

Standing there in the cold Montana wind, the scrub grass rippling in the force of the gale, Dakota's hair whipping out to the side, her lips plump from his kiss, he had to agree that "wow" pretty much covered it. He'd never been affected by a kiss like that before, feeling it all the way down to his toes.

"We'd better get back on patrol," she said quickly, moving toward Barney.

"Dakota."

She turned, her cheeks pink with what might have been embarrassment; he wasn't sure. He just didn't want it to end like this, with embarrassment or retreat. That kiss had meant something—maybe something neither of them had a right to, but it had still meant something.

"You don't have to be nervous being alone with me."

She didn't need to be jerked around or to have her emotions go through the wringer. She certainly didn't need to be uncomfortable around him for the rest of the drive. He'd look out for her and make sure that no one gave her any trouble. Beyond that, he wasn't planning on sticking around Hope, and he knew better than to toy with a good woman. He'd kissed her, and she'd kissed him back, but she didn't owe him anything.

"Okay." She nodded.

"I won't do that again."

A long, low howl echoed across the plains, but wind whipped the sound into a tangle so that he couldn't tell the direction it was coming from. The horses danced nervously.

"We'd better get moving," she said. "There are wolves out there."

He wasn't sure if she was referring the howling beasts in the distance or the ones closer to home that betrayed her trust, but Dakota was safe with him, even if that meant restraining himself from doing the one thing he wanted most right now—kissing her all over again. As they mounted their horses once more, the first stinging pellets of rain began to fall.

Chapter Eight

It rained for the most of the night and when Dakota awoke the next morning to the sound of voices, her body ached from the previous day's work. She rolled out of her warm sleeping bag, fully dressed, and pulled on her jacket, zipping it up with a shiver. As she unzipped her tent and stepped outside, she sucked in a deep breath of cold morning air.

That kiss last night had happened—something she'd questioned a couple of times before morning. She and Andy had done the rest of the patrol together and, after rubbing down their horses, Andy had paused with her in the darkness.

"What's that old rhyme? If wishes were horses...?" His voice was low and soft in her ear.

"Beggars would ride." She finished the line.

His hand brushed against hers, his fingers moving lightly down hers, ever so close to entwining them together.

"Ever wish you had a do-over?" he asked quietly. "Ever wish you could go back and make a different choice and see how your life would have turned out?"

Dakota thought for a moment then slowly shook her head. "I wouldn't be the same woman I am today."

He nodded slowly. "That's a good thing, to live without regrets."

"What about you?" she whispered.

"I guess that leaves me a beggar who dreams of riding." He touched her cheek with the back of his finger. "Good night, Dakota."

What had he meant by that? She had a feeling he had a few unfulfilled wishes of his own. Heaven knew she did. But wishes weren't enough for ambitions or for the heart—and old nursery rhymes strove to teach the children that very truth. Wishes got you nowhere. Hard work, on the other hand, produced something.

When she'd crawled into her sleeping bag, she'd lain there for a long time, remembering the feel of his lips on hers. She'd never imagined kissing Andy Granger would feel quite so sweet. His first kiss had made her feel safe, and the second had awakened feelings inside her she'd thought were dormant. The memory warmed her in spite of the damp weather.

But the cocoon of night had evaporated and morning came as it always did. The rain had stopped, but everything was drenched and the sunrise looked more like a silver haze than the actual start of a day. Harley had managed to get a smoky fire started, but it wouldn't last long if it started raining again. Fog rolled along the scrub grass, the cows looking like shadows in the mist. Dakota's breath hung in the air

and she rubbed her hands together against the chill.
She looked around the camp and spotted Andy with
the horses under a tarp. He hoisted the saddle up
onto Romeo's back.

"Morning," Andy said. "How'd you sleep?"

"Not great," she admitted.

"My fault?" he asked, warm eyes meeting hers.

She felt the blush rise in her cheeks but before she
could answer, he added, "We're starting early today,
before the rain hits us."

"Okay," she said. "I'll be ready."

He turned back to buckling straps and adjusting
the saddle. He hadn't known about Dwight's violent
streak—hadn't even suspected—and that had been
reassuring. He'd made her feel safe last night. De-
sired. He'd gotten right past all of her bravado and
when his lips came down onto hers…that was something she hadn't allowed a man to do since Dwight.
But none of those feelings changed how her family
felt about Andy, and her loyalty had to be to them
first. Even if Andy wasn't the jerk they all believed
him to be, he was still the reason her father con-
stantly worried about losing his land. They wouldn't
understand; they'd be furious.

All she was certain of right now was that Andy
had kissed her and she'd kissed him back.

Dakota took down her tent. The other drovers
emerged from their own soon after and followed suit.
It didn't take long to load up the pack horses and they
ate a quick breakfast of leftover biscuits and hot coffee as they worked. They all stashed what they could

to carry with them for later—their next proper meal wouldn't be until evening. The sooner they got the cattle across the river, the sooner they could head toward home, where they could dry out and get paid.

And getting paid was the point of this whole trip. For some reason she kept forgetting that. As she mounted her horse again that morning, Andy caught her eye with a small smile before easing his horse forward.

The kiss had meant something to him, it seemed, and she felt a wave of uncertainty. Feeling anything at all for Andy hadn't been part of the plan, and she couldn't help but remember her words to her mother that she could handle Andy Granger. She felt like a fraud. What was it about the open land that changed people?

The next hour the fog dissipated and the sky brightened, although the clouds hung low and refused to be pushed away. Dakota warmed up the best way she knew how—with work, and they herded the cattle and brought them to the river's edge. The river had swelled over night from the deluge of rain and it thundered between the banks in a brown, broiling swell. It had obviously rained up in the mountains, as well, and crossing the river again wasn't going to be as easy as the first time. Dakota looked toward Andy and saw the same expression of concern on his face. She kicked her horse into motion and cantered closer.

"Will we make it across?" she asked, raising her voice above the whistle of the wind.

A mist of light rain blew into her face and her

horse pranced beneath her, anxious to get moving again.

"We'll have to try," he said and then raised his voice so the other drovers could hear him. "Okay, boys, let's get rolling!"

That was all they needed. The drovers started doing what they did best—whooping and shouting and pushing the herd from behind until the first cows were nudged forward and they plunged into the water and started the manic swim for the opposite shore. When the lead few made it to the middle, the rest tumbled into the water after them and for a long while the water was filled with mooing, bawling, thrashing, writhing life.

When they made it to the other bank, the cattle stumbled and scrambled to get a foothold in the mud before pulling themselves onto the land, being pushed forward from behind. They ran into the opposite field, dripping dirty water, their wide bodies streaked with mud.

So far the cattle were all making it across safely. There had been a few close calls when some of the large calves had struggled to keep up with their mothers, but they'd made it in the end, and Dakota breathed a sigh of relief. Losing cattle on the drive wasn't something a drover took pride in, and she felt compassion for the cattle, too. They were gentle creatures and a lost calf or comrade would be hard on them.

Dave and Finn crossed the river as the herd on their side began to thin out, leading the remaining cattle by example. Elliot, Harley, Andy and Dakota stayed behind, urging the cattle forward and into the water. It was a team effort and the hardest part of the drive by far.

An hour slid by as Dakota whooped and herded, Barney's hooves slipping in the mud as she pulled him around to cut off an escaping steer.

Overhead a peal of thunder boomed and for a moment she heard nothing but ringing in her ears. Only a few cows were left on the bank of the river— cows and the smallest of the calves. As the thunder exploded, the cows turned and stampeded away from the water, heading for the distant tree line, their calves trailing behind.

Andy wheeled his horse around and Dakota followed his example, hooves pounding as they raced after the fleeing cows. Dakota leaned low as Barney galloped ahead of the cows, then she pulled him around and cut off the leader. Andy did the same for a steer and soon they had the cows stopped and mooing in frustration. There were at least seventy or eighty adult cows and nine of the smallest calves, and as they herded them back toward the river, Andy shot her a grin.

"You're really good at this," he said.

"Told you." She laughed. "This is the fun part."

"You keep saying."

Harley was waiting for them at the river's edge, his attention focused on the swirling water. When Andy and Dakota arrived behind the protesting cattle, Dakota could see the problem. The banks had collapsed from the hooves of three-hundred-odd cows and the onslaught of water hadn't abated. The adult cows might make it across the river, but the calves didn't have a chance. On the other side, the drovers had herded the cattle into a closer unit, waiting for Andy's orders.

"Boss!" Finn shouted. "What's the plan?"

The plan. Anyone raised in the country knew that there had to be a plan. Nothing worked without one. Wishes and dreams had no place on a ranch. From a distance, grazing cattle and peaceful scenery might seem pastoral and relaxing, but a rancher never relaxed. She was always looking at the next step, preparing for the next season, the next hurdle.

If wishes were horses...

In her experience, wishes were a waste of time. If wishes held any kind of clout with local government instead of that blasted Lordship Land Developers... If wishes were dollars... If wishes could hydrate a parched field... If wishes could bring Brody home safely... If wishes could change her family's view of this complicated man in front of her... Wishes didn't count for much.

Andy looked over at Dakota, green eyes meeting hers in a silent request. He needed her advice and, right now, she was the one he trusted.

"The calves won't make it," Dakota said, keeping her tone low. "We can either wait it out here or go downstream and see if we can find a shallower spot. It's your call."

Andy nodded, was silent for a beat and then raised

his voice. "We're going to take these downstream and see if we can find some shallower water for the calves. Carry on toward the camp. Lydia and Bob will be there tonight, and if we don't join you by morning, send someone."

"Sure thing!" Finn shouted back. "Good luck!"

The drovers on the opposite bank turned away and Dakota pushed her hat more firmly onto her head, pulling her chin down to protect her face from the driving drizzle.

If wishes were horses, Dwight would never have started drinking and she'd be married right now with a few kids of her own. And maybe that would have been good enough, even if Dwight had never aroused the kind of passion inside her that Andy seemed to manage last night. It would have been the life she'd always pictured, and she wouldn't be facing all these challenges and complications by herself.

She had her family, and that counted for a whole lot, except her family had no idea she'd kissed the enemy and that she was empathizing with Andy in spite of her best intentions. When it came to Andy, she was one hundred percent alone.

And, ironically, when it came to life in Hope, so was Andy.

THE SKY CLEARED the farther they rode downstream and by the time midmorning arrived, sunlight beamed down on the sodden countryside, making the drops of water shine like diamonds. Copses of leafless trees lined the banks of the river, some trees

leaning heavily toward the water but still miracu-
lously staying rooted as the rush of water ate away
at the earthen banks. The cows trotted complacently
ahead of them. A blue jay squawked overhead, followed by the twitter of smaller birds. These were
the kinds of scenes he was afraid to let himself miss.

Back in Billings he'd sit in his office, focused on
quarterly sales figures, and in some corner of his
mind he'd remember some breathtaking view he'd
witnessed on horseback—just sitting there in the
middle of nowhere, drinking in a sun-splashed vista.
This one could be filed with the others—scenes so
lovely they ached when you remembered them from
the confines of a city office.

Andy looked over to Dakota, but her gaze was
fixed straight in front of her.

He shouldn't have kissed her.

He was letting himself feel things he shouldn't be
feeling. Hope was supposed to be a pit stop while he
helped out his brother and tried to somehow make
up for selling the family land out from under him.
Reigniting old emotional attachments wasn't part of
the plan. Yet the more time he spent with Dakota,
the more attached he was getting, which meant that
kissing her had been a monumental mistake.

The three of them easily kept the cattle moving,
and Harley rode a good distance from Andy and Dakota, leaving them in relative privacy. Andy wanted
to talk to her, but he couldn't say the things that
were on his mind, namely that she sparked something inside him that he'd never felt before, even with

Ida. Dakota made him wish for things and hope for things, but she was as much a part of this land as his brother was, and he knew what that meant.

The Grangers put family and the land ahead of everything else, and sometimes the top priority was blurry. You couldn't separate Chet from the land without tearing off a part of him. Andy had made that separation, but it hadn't been easy.

Dakota, he knew, was the same as his brother, and feeling things for her wasn't smart. She'd put her family and that land above anything else she might be feeling. He was neither family nor sticking around, so allowing himself to feel whatever it was he was feeling for Dakota was masochistic at best. Yet he couldn't stop remembering the sight of her in the darkness. It wasn't just that she was beautiful—he'd been around beautiful women before. It was more than that—it was the way he softened around her, the way he wanted to protect her, to defend her. She was so much more than just a beautiful woman, and when he thought about the way her glittering eyes met his, how her lips parted ever so slightly—

"Do you ever talk to my brother on Facebook or anything?"

Andy's reverie popped at the sound of her voice and he dragged his mind back to present.

"Sorry?" he asked.

"Brody. You aren't connected on social media, are you? I mean, through friends of friends, or something like that."

"Uh...no." Brody had been a couple of years older

and he'd hung out with a different group. Brody been in Chet's graduating class, but even so, he'd hung out with a different group of kids than Chet had.

"Okay, well...that's good."

"Why's that?" Andy asked with a short laugh.

Her gaze flickered toward him and he sensed her discomfort. Was he really such an embarrassment that she wanted to hide him from her brother, too?

"It's nothing," she said.

That was a lie—he could see it written all over her face.

"Why? Is Brody going to have a problem with you doing this cattle drive with me?" he asked.

"He can't stand you, but that's not the point." She shot him a quirky smile.

She certainly didn't sugarcoat it, did she? But no one in Hope liked him right now, so it didn't come as a surprise. Besides, it was Brody's ranch, too, that had been decimated by his sale. Regardless, Andy respected the guy—he was fighting for his country, after all—and the truth of Brody's opinion stung a little.

"I'm doing damage control," she said.

"For what?"

"He doesn't know about Nina yet."

This was one bit of gossip he *had* heard all the way in Billings. It was such a small-town-drama kind of thing to happen that Andy had been bitterly amused. But he no longer had to care—his life was in Billings. It felt different now, though, looking Dakota in the face.

"You didn't tell him?" he asked after a moment.

"No."

"Why?"

She turned away, letting out a sharp whistle that got a cow moving again, then glanced in his direction again.

"Because when he deployed, he was engaged. And then one day, a few months after Brody had left, I saw Nina making out with Brian Dickerson in the back of a movie theater. I was pretty shocked. I mean, I'd never been a huge fan of her for a sister-in-law, but..."

"Did you say anything to her?" he asked.

"I didn't have to. We looked at each other, she turned beet red, and I left." Dakota smiled but it didn't reach her eyes. "That evening Nina called me to explain. She said she didn't think she could wait for Brody to come back. My parents were the ones who came up with the plan, though."

"Which was to hide it from Brody?" Andy clarified. It looked like Brody had the same kind of family he did—the kind that pulled together so hard, they could crack a nut with the sheer force of their good intentions.

"They didn't want to spring it on him while he's dodging bullets. He'll be home in February and we'll tell him then."

"He hasn't noticed on social media or anything?" Andy asked incredulously.

"We talked to his friends and they agreed to go along with it," she said.

"And Nina?" he asked.

"She got off social media completely—the only way to really keep this private. She answers his emails as briefly as possible, because she owes us this much. She can't crush him—not now. He'll face reality when he's home again."

"And you don't think Brody will be pissed?" he asked.

Dakota's face paled. He'd hit on it, he could tell. Brody would absolutely be angry when he got back. So that was the kind of family the Masons were: well-intentioned and so determined that they'd managed to get every single one of Brody's friends and family to portray a lie. That took a massive force of will. They took care of their own to the extreme. He had a feeling Brody was going to be boiling mad when he got home and found out what had really been going on.

"Are you judging me?" she asked. "He could get killed over there, Andy. I'd rather deal with him being angry if it means getting him home alive."

Andy shrugged. He could see the point, albeit grudgingly. "I get it. I'm not sure he will, though."

"I've been thinking the same thing," she said, her tone softening. "I'm not sure I can keep doing this."

"No?"

"I mean, the last email I sent him I told him about doing this cattle drive with you. Once I get back, I expect that you'll monopolize conversation for a bit." She winced. "He really doesn't like you. I'm just not sure how much longer you'll be a distraction."

"A distraction." He shot her an irritated look. "Is that what I am to you?"

Was that all he was, at this point? He'd thought they'd gotten to know each other over the last few days. He thought he'd been able to show her who he was underneath all the scandal associated with him. In fact, they'd gotten a whole lot closer than that.

Color rose in her cheeks. "When it comes to emailing my brother, yes."

He wasn't sure what he expected her to say, but not that. He was tired of being the bad guy, the black sheep, the prodigal son. He was sick of being glared at and ignored, worrying about the meals he ordered in local diners. He'd thought he'd been able to crack through all of that with Dakota, and the color in her cheeks suggested she was feeling more than she was saying.

"After last night, you don't think we count as friends yet?" he demanded. There was no point in dancing around it anymore. They'd shared something special, however fleeting it might be. The memory of her slender waist, the feel of her straining up toward his mouth, the way she'd melted into his embrace, the perfect fit... It was all he'd been thinking about all day.

"I don't want to talk about that."

"Why not?" He pressed on. "If you didn't want me to kiss you, you can say so. I'm not pushing myself on you."

He hadn't pushed her into that kiss. It had been

very mutual, and the memory of her in his arms sped up his heart even now.

"I'm no wilting flower. If I hadn't wanted to kiss you, I wouldn't have. But—"

"But we've made it a little past friendly," he said, keeping his voice low.

Her cheeks turned pink. "I don't think we meant to do that."

She was right. He hadn't. Feeling things for her wasn't in the plan, and if he could put a brake on what he was feeling, he would. Heck, he was trying to. But that kiss had been real, and he was pretty sure they'd both felt it.

"My family hates you, Andy."

"Yep," he agreed, keeping his eyes on the cattle. He completely understood. The Masons weren't a family to trifle with. If he wanted something with her—really wanted it—then this Granger had just met his match in difficult families.

"And you're not staying." She couldn't hide the regret in those words, but she was right, he couldn't stay.

"Hope won't forgive me," he said, hearing the sadness in his own voice. "You're right. I'm headed back to Billings as soon as I can."

"So maybe what happens on the trail can stay on the trail," she said quietly.

"Don't worry, your secret is safe with me," he said.

"Which one?" she asked.

"All of it. I'm not here to make your life any harder." He looked over at her and caught her gaze for a moment. If things had been different, he wouldn't walk away so easily, but he was a practical man. He clicked his tongue and Romeo sped up at the command. "As for Brody, I say tell him. He's no idiot. I'm sure he suspects something already."

"Okay." Her voice stayed quiet. "Thanks."

For his discretion about their kiss or his advice? Maybe it didn't matter. This—the feelings sparking between them, the hopes he kept trying to slap back down—wouldn't last. Soon enough they'd return to civilization again and Dakota would slip back into her life. She was a Mason, and her family would have other hopes for her that didn't include their arch nemesis. Whatever was growing between them right now could never survive Hope's scrutiny.

Andy eased his horse forward, breaking into a trot to head off a wandering calf. They'd gone from civil to slipping past friendship in the matter of one night. It hadn't been planned. In fact, if he'd been thinking straight, he would never have done it, but there was something about those chocolate-brown eyes and the direct way she stared at him that emptied his head of logical thought.

Do the cattle drive and get out—that had been the plan. When exactly had it gotten more complicated?

Chapter Nine

The river's swell had started to decrease as evening came on and, after some debate, they decided to set up camp. Getting eighty head across a river at twilight wasn't going to be easy, and in the morning, if the river had gone down even further, they'd be in a much better situation to get across safely. Their food, what they'd been able to carry with them, had been mostly eaten, and Dakota was thinking of the rest of the group who would be arriving at their own camp at the same time—except they'd have Lydia Granger's savory cooking to welcome them.

The hoot of an owl drew Dakota's attention and she watched as the shadow swept across the field then disappeared into some trees. The evening air was cold, chilling quickly as the last of the sun vanished behind the mountains, leaving behind a dusky sky edged with red along the silhouette of the range.

This would be an uncomfortable night. No tents. No bedding. No blankets. No shelter from the elements. Fortunately, Harley proved talented at starting another bonfire, and when they all rummaged in their saddle bags, they came up with some dried fruit, a handful of nuts, two sticks of beef jerky and six granola bars.

"This will be an interesting meal," she laughed, tossing her granola bars onto the pile.

"We have to cross tomorrow morning," Andy said. "No choice. We'll have to take our chances."

Dakota had to agree. They weren't exactly set up for a lengthy stay out here, and the weather was only getting colder.

"At least the rain has stopped," Harley said from his position by the fire. He was steadily feeding the flames pine cones and old twigs, patiently building the smoking blaze.

A fallen log lay close by the fire and proved to be a convenient seat. Andy came and sat next to her, his arm an inch away from hers—close enough she found herself instinctively wanting to lean into him. What was it about Andy that made her respond like this? Normally she had her wits about her. Even with Dwight, she'd been able to pull herself together and break it off with him permanently because she could see that he was no good for her. Well, Andy wasn't much good for her, either—not if she wanted an actual future with a man—and yet she still found herself drawn to him. She glanced over and Andy smiled back, those green eyes enveloping her for a moment of warmth before he turned his attention to Harley.

"So how long are you planning on staying around Hope?" Andy asked.

Harley put another stick on the fire and leaned

back on his haunches. "Don't know. As long as it takes, I guess."

"Your sister, you mean," Andy clarified.

Harley didn't look the least bit surprised that Andy knew about his personal business. Instead he reached for his pile of food, giving Dakota a nod of thanks.

"Yeah, that's right," he said. "You all might be partial to Elliot, but I'm not."

"Your sister seems to be," Dakota said with a shrug. If she'd chosen to stay with him, there must be something keeping her there. "Maybe she's happy."

Harley tore off a bite of beef jerky and chewed silent for a minute. Then he shook his head. "Do you have any siblings?"

"A brother," she said.

"And if you settled for some guy—let go of all the things that mattered to you and went off with some cowboy who had no respect for you or your family, do you think he'd have a problem with it?"

An image of Brody rose in her mind and she wondered what he'd say if he told him she was dating Andy Granger. He'd have a whole lot to say, she was sure. Just as he had when he'd found out what Dwight had been doing to her. Brothers were protective in a unique way, and if he ever found out what had blossomed between her and Andy on this drive, she wouldn't want to face him. So, would Brody have a problem with her settling for someone the family hated?

"Probably," she said with a short laugh. "But what

if I loved that cowboy? What if I didn't want to give him up? There wouldn't be a whole lot he could do."

She was feeling defiant right now, protective of this other woman's choice to choose her future because it mirrored her own situation right now…in a small way, at least. She shouldn't take it so personally. She wasn't in love with Andy and she certainly wasn't pregnant. Harley had a solid point about Elliot's bad behavior. She didn't even know why she felt this need to get involved.

"She's my twin." Harley said it as if ended the discussion.

Dakota frowned. "But she's still her own person."

"Of course!" Harley barked out a laugh. "Any man who tries to control a country woman is either stupid or has a death wish! I'm not saying that I have any right to dictate her life. I'm saying I *know* her. She's my twin sister and I know her better than anyone. She's pregnant, she feels guilty for that, and she's sticking by the man who got her into that situation."

"What happened, exactly?" Andy asked.

"She brought him home for the weekend, announced she was having a baby, and Elliot just sat there. He was the father, but he didn't make any move to reassure us that he'd take care of her. My mom suggested they get married, and Holly wanted that. She lit up at the mention of a wedding. My mom still has my great-grandmother's wedding dress, and Holly always dreamed of wearing that dress down the aisle. That wedding—it mattered to *her*. Elliot got all dark and quiet. He wasn't going to give her the wedding she wanted—I could see it in his face. And while I think that kids need both their parents, and dads matter a heck of a lot, I don't think a woman should have to stay with a man who commits only as far as a rent check. She deserves the real thing, and Elliot ain't it."

Dakota had to agree with the kid there. If Holly wanted marriage, then sharing the bills wasn't going to be commitment enough. It wouldn't be for Dakota, either. She wondered what Holly's take on all of this was.

Andy didn't say anything and he looked away, elbows on his knees and hands hanging down between. He didn't seem to be listening, his attention diverted by something inside him.

"And the family..." Harley went on quietly. "Well, we can't just forgive him. He doesn't think that Holly is worth marrying, and we happen to disagree something fierce. Holly is pretty great, and I'm not going to stand by while she puts up with less than she's worth because she's feeling guilty about an unplanned pregnancy. We were raised with church and all that, so there were expectations. But we all carry regrets in some form or other, and it's no excuse for giving up."

Dakota looked toward the cattle. A nearby cow chewed its cud in slow revolutions, big, watery eyes fixed on them as if they were interesting to her. Her half-grown calf lay next to her, curled into a ball and fast asleep. The cows always made life seem so much less complicated somehow. Everything could be solved, given enough time, enough thought.

"So what do you plan to do about it?" Andy asked after a moment.

"I'm going to talk to her."

"I thought you did already," Dakota said, pulling her attention back to the conversation.

"No, I got kicked out. That's not a conversation. That's shutting down." Harley shook his head. "I won't clear out until she and I have sat down together and talked. Until then, I'm sticking around."

Dakota felt mildly sorry for Holly. Explaining herself to her family wasn't going to be easy, and in this Dakota could empathize. She had a tight family, too, and the thing with tight families was that while you could always count on them to be there for you, they also expected something in return—transparency. You didn't get to crawl into a hole to figure out how you were feeling, because they'd dig you right out and demand an explanation. They worried. They tried to help. In Holly's situation, they'd followed her all the way to Hope. Sometimes a girl didn't want to admit that she had no idea how she felt or that she didn't have a plan yet. Sometimes a girl just wanted to hunker down and lick her wounds. Holly wasn't going to get that freedom.

There was one thing she was certain of, however, and that was that Elliot had his own sense of pride, and Harley's presence had wounded it. Ranch wisdom said you should never back something meaner than you into a corner, and frankly, Elliot was the meaner of the two.

She sighed. "You think Elliot is going to be okay with all of that?"

"Quite honestly," Harley replied, "I don't think he cares all that much about keeping her."

Maybe Harley was right and maybe he was dead wrong. Every act of betrayal—and if Harley broke up his sister's relationship, she'd most definitely see it as betrayal—seemed to start with only the best of intentions. *I was only trying to help.*

Harley had good intentions and she could understand those good intentions, because her family had the same good intentions. They took care of their own, too. They tramped over boundaries and dug people out of their holes and helped them whether they liked it or not. That's what family did—and, hopefully, you lived to appreciate it.

Dakota could only hope that Brody would understand that, because whether she came clean now or two months from now when March rolled 'round and Brody came home on leave, she was still part of that deception—at the very heart of it. And Brody would see what they'd done as a betrayal, too.

HARLEY TOOK THE first patrol that night. He hummed to himself as he cantered off into the darkness, his voice mingled with the soft lowing of the cattle. He had a surprisingly smooth baritone and he sang an old Christmas carol that tugged at Andy's heart. "It

Came Upon a Midnight Clear"—one of his mother's favorites.

Beside him, Dakota shivered, and Andy moved closer and put his arm around her. She startled.

"Just keeping you warm," he said.

She leaned into him, fitting neatly under his arm, and they both sat in silence for a long time, listening to Harley's voice as he sang to the cattle on his rounds.

"What were you thinking about?" Dakota asked, rubbing her hands together.

"When?" he asked.

"When Harley was talking about his sister," she said. "You got this faraway look in your eye."

"Oh." Had she noticed that? He'd thought he'd managed to hide his feelings, but apparently not from her. He shrugged. "I'm not much better than Elliot."

"What?" She laughed and shook her head. "I think you might be too hard on yourself."

"I was with Ida for four years before we broke up," he said. "She wanted to get married and I—" His mind went back to the life he'd shared with Ida in Billings. She'd been a good woman—there was no denying that. He'd proposed, but he'd also had a hundred good excuses to keep putting that wedding off. "I knew she was a really great woman and, in theory, I couldn't do better, but I wasn't sure about marrying her. So instead of proposing, I asked her to move in with me. We lived together for a year before I proposed, but I wasn't in any hurry to get married. It didn't feel right."

"You broke up pretty close to the wedding, didn't you?" she asked quietly.

"Yeah." He nodded. "And the main issue was that I'd never really wanted to get married—not like she had. And Ida figured that out. She was smart enough to call it off because she didn't want to be married to someone who didn't want to be there heart and soul."

Dakota leaned forward toward the fire and he let his arm drop away from her shoulder.

"Breakups happen, Andy."

"They do, but I should have been man enough to face what I was really feeling. Instead of dodging marriage by asking her to move in with me, I should have told her the truth. Elliot's not a bad guy, but he's doing the same thing I did—dodging a marriage he doesn't want deep down. And that ends up hurting everyone."

He glanced toward her, expecting to see judgment on her face, but instead he found her watching him. Her expression was sad and gentle.

"I don't know, Andy," she said. "Marrying the wrong woman would have been a far sight worse."

He smiled. "You're quite pragmatic, aren't you?"

"A cattlewoman has to be." She shot him a grin. "You're a good guy, Andy. That's the thing—you hide it well. You manage to convince everyone that you don't care, but you do. And you're a better man than you pretend to be."

A good guy. Dakota, who never minced words and always saw through him, saw some good. It softened him and he cleared his throat, looking away.

"Coming from you, that's high praise," he said ruefully.

"Flattery is a time waster." She pushed a half-burned stick back into the fire.

Elliot might not be able to stand him, but Andy could empathize with the rugged cowboy because he'd been there. Maybe Andy had been a little more polished, but the drive was the same. When it wasn't the right fit, a man dreaded getting hitched. And now Elliot had a baby on the way to complicate things further. What if he'd gotten Ida pregnant? He'd have married her, of course, and done the right thing by her. He'd have raised his family. But that wouldn't have changed the fact that they weren't the right match. They lacked that unexplainable spark that really great couples seemed to have—couples like Chet and Mackenzie, like Ida and Calvin.

The fire popped an explosion of sparks and Andy leaned forward to put another bundle of sticks onto the blaze. The wind was getting colder and it whistled through the trees in a low moan. No one would get much sleep tonight. As he settled back next to Dakota, he slid his arm around her again, nudging her closer. She followed his encouragement and settled against his side. She felt good tucked under his arm like that, like she was made for it. There was something about having Dakota next to him that made him more alert, more aware of his surroundings. The wind whipped up again, leaves swirling and the fire nearly going out before the wind changed direction again.

Dakota shivered.

"Cold?" he murmured.

She nodded and he rubbed his hand over her jacketed arm. Andy would be surprised if there wasn't snow in the morning. She leaned her head against his shoulder and when he leaned his cheek against the top of her head he could feel the silkiness of her hair against his three-day stubble.

Back in Hope, he'd been faced with public opinion about his mistakes, and no one seemed terribly interested in understanding his side of things. *A good guy.* They could have been empty words, meant only to be polite, except Dakota had never been the type to offer empty platitudes. That was one of the things he respected about her.

"Did you mean it?" he asked quietly.

"Hmm?" She straightened and looked up at him.

"You honestly think I'm a good guy, in spite of it all?" he asked quietly. "I'm the rat who sold out, you remember."

She met his gaze evenly. "You're a good man, Andy."

She wiped a hair away from her face and she was so close that he could feel the warmth of her breath against his cheek. Neither of them moved away. He'd always trusted Dakota to see through him and he realized there was nothing quite so comforting as having a woman see right down to the heart of him. His gaze flickered from her brown eyes down to her pink lips and, before he could think better of it, he lowered his lips onto hers.

She wasn't surprised this time when he kissed her, and she leaned into him. He cupped her face with one hand and pulled her closer still with the other. The kiss quickly deepened as she moved against him, closing the cold out as his heart sped up to meet hers. He knew they shouldn't be doing this again, but for the life of him he couldn't remember why against the blood pounding in his ears.

Dakota put a hand against his chest and pushed him back. She sucked in a breath and laughed shakily.

"We've got to stop doing that."

"Yeah, we do," he agreed, closing his eyes, willing his blood to calm. "Sorry about that."

"It was me, too," she said.

Far away, they could hear Harley's voice singing "Oh, Come All Ye Faithful." His mom had liked that one, too. Every Christmas Eve she'd insisted they go to church, and those old carols had shaken that little church with the fervent voices of friends and neighbors.

"I'm feeling things I haven't felt before," he admitted after a moment. "I know it's no help, and it's not possible, but I've never felt—" He swallowed.

"Me, too." She pulled back and he dropped his hands. She felt too far away. "We should stop this before someone gets hurt, Andy."

He knew she was right. This couldn't work for a hundred different reasons. Why was it that the women who were available and appropriate didn't do this to him, but the one woman completely out of reach made his head empty of every logical thought, made him want to hold her again, no matter the consequences to his heart later on? In the moment, it always seemed worth it.

But she was right. If they didn't have a future, they were tormenting themselves for nothing, and while he might be willing to risk his own torment, he wasn't willing to risk hers.

"My family will never accept you," she said quietly, as if reading his mind.

Was she trying to think of a way to make it work? Or was that just wishful thinking on his part? But he knew better than to ask her to cross that line. That step outside the family circle tended to be a permanent one. When he'd sold that land and gone to Billings, it had solidified something that had been in process for years. The once malleable boundaries hardened and he was officially an outsider. Was he still a Granger? In name, maybe.

"I think I understand why Holly doesn't want to go home," Andy said, trying to pull his thoughts together again. "There are points in your life, steps that you take, that change you. There isn't any going back. Harley wants her to go home, but maybe she knows better. Maybe she knows that the door is already closed and it'll never be the same again."

"Like you," she whispered.

"Yeah, like me." He gave her a sad smile. "It can be lonely out here on the outside."

She slid her hand into his and he squeezed her fingers, listening to Harley's distant singing.

"My mom used to sing that song," Andy said softly. "She was a real stickler for the real meaning of Christmas and all that."

"You're missing her," she said.

"I miss her most at Christmas." He inhaled deeply. "It's funny, though. She made sure I knew about the angels and the wise men and the baby in the stable. That mattered to her because it was what Christmas was all about in our home. Even when she was dying, when she'd ask us to sing carols with her, she believed. Oh, how she believed. She was going to a better place. But for me—" his voice broke and he swallowed hard "—the meaning of Christmas for me was listening to the angels in *her* voice. I was a boy losing his mother."

Dakota tipped her head onto his shoulder. "Don't you keep any of the traditions in her memory?"

"One," he admitted. "My mom used to hang mistletoe around the house when we were kids, and you'd have to walk around watching the ceiling, because she kept moving it. And if you stopped anywhere around the mistletoe, she'd descend on you and smother you with kisses."

"That's so sweet."

"Yeah." He smiled at the memory. "I'd put up a fight for appearances, but I liked it. Do you know what it's like to be loved by someone that fiercely? When she died, I lost seventy-five percent of the love in my life in one fell swoop. So I hang mistletoe in my apartment in Billings," he said. "For her."

He could see tears in her eyes. She wrapped her

arms around herself and when he squeezed her hand, she met his gaze again.

"Keep your foot in the door," he said softly. "I can't ask you to give up your family. I wouldn't be much of a man if I did that. When the ones who love you are gone, you realize just how much you lost."

What he wanted to do was to take advantage of these last couple of hours of privacy, pull her into his arms and show her exactly how she made him feel, but that would be selfish. It would comfort him in the moment, but at her expense.

Besides, once they returned to Hope, it would be harder to then have her realize anything between them had only been a fantasy, instead of seeing it now. It would hurt more to watch the realization dawn on her, to watch the change in her eyes when she looked at him.

He didn't want to mess with her heart but, frankly, he had a heart to protect, too. And while Andy had been able to break things off with other women without too much scarring, he knew for a fact that Dakota would be a different story, and no man walked into that willingly.

Chapter Ten

Half a mile downstream the river widened and slowed—the perfect place for eighty head of cattle to get across, and when the sun was still low and golden, Dakota ignored the empty gnaw in her stomach as they herded the cattle through the hip-deep water to the other side. Morning brought frost, covering the countryside in white lace that crept back as the sun warmed the ground. Their breath hung in the air and, as the morning progressed, Dakota was grateful for the warmth of the sun on her shoulders.

The night hadn't been a restful one. They'd kept the fire going and leaned against each other for support and warmth. Leaning against Andy had made her feel more of the same things she didn't want to feel. Hating him was easier. As was judging him. But understanding his perspective and realizing their attraction to each other was both mutual and powerful—that was difficult.

When Andy went on patrol, she'd lain next to the fire, and she and Harley had attempted to get some sleep. They'd need any rest so they could manage the long day coming. And when Dakota took her turn at patrol, she'd been relieved to have some solitude to try to sort out the anxiety that wormed up inside her.

They got up and saddled their horses the next morning. There was no breakfast, no coffee, and they all wanted to get moving as quickly as possible. The sooner they started out, the sooner they'd get back to the rest of the group—and food.

Things were getting complicated and she knew it. While they were out on the drive, she could push aside all the other burdens and expectations waiting for her back at the ranch, but the closer they got to home, the less she could ignore it all. She was falling for the cowboy who'd ruined her family's land.

"We'll be home tomorrow," Andy said. "Back to normal."

Normal. Did she really want everything to be normal again? Normal included a massive family secret they'd been hiding from her brother. It included her father's heavy heart as he struggled to make ends meet on a ranch that was costing more and more to run. Normal also meant being alone—no stolen kisses, no leaning into that space underneath Andy's arm that was the warmest nook she'd ever found. Normal certainly came with a price.

"We'll both be busy, I'm sure," she said. And they would be. She'd be working with their own cattle. She had a line of fencing to fix and she and her mother had plans to build a new chicken coop before winter. And then there was Brody...

She hadn't decided yet how she'd deal with him.

She'd never forgive herself if she went against the family plan and he died over there. She took off her hat and pulled her hand through her hair. It would feel good to get home and shower.

The freedom to feel all these tumultuous feelings would come to an end in precisely two days, and they'd be back to obligation and responsibility. They'd be back to "normal."

"About Dwight…" Andy said. "I'm going to have a talk with him before I leave."

"Don't bother," she said with a shake of her head. "I'm fine."

"Who said it was for you?" he retorted.

When she looked over at him, she saw a teasing smile on his lips.

"That's all over now," she said, rolling her eyes. "Let it go."

"Thing is," Andy said, "he lied to me."

"What are you talking about?"

Ahead of them, Harley kicked his horse into a trot to head off a wandering cow and Dakota looked at Andy. The joking was gone from his face and his jaw was clenched. The morning sun glistened on the auburn stubble on his chin and when his gaze cut toward her, she felt warmth rising in her cheeks.

"When I asked you out and you turned me down, Dwight told me that you and he were starting things up, and I understood that. I did the honorable thing and backed off." He shot her a rueful smile. "Well, I didn't think you'd actually choose me over him, anyway. If I thought I had a chance, I probably would have been significantly less honorable. You always saw right through my attempts to be cool and collected. What can I say?"

"So when did he lie?" she asked.

"When I told him that he was a lucky guy because a girl like you—" He shook his head, started again. "You were the kind of girl who walked her own path, wasn't afraid of anything. You were special. So I told him that I'd totally back off. No hard feelings. I just wanted him to take care of you. Be good to you. You deserved that."

Dakota felt tears mist her eyes and she quickly looked away. His words had managed to slip right beneath her defenses. She hadn't realized there had been any competition going on between Andy and Dwight back then. She'd thought Dwight was the decent one and Andy was the flirt. It had all been so black and white. So simple.

"He said he would," Andy went on, his voice low. "But he didn't keep his word, now, did he? So I have a few things to settle with Dwight on my own. We were buddies. I backed off. He didn't keep his end of that bargain."

Several cows slowed to a stop and Andy pulled his horse away and went after them. She watched him go, her mind whirling. How much had she missed back then with her steel-clad certainty about how things stood? She'd always been opinionated and she wasn't easy to sway, but in that situation she'd been wrong. Dwight wasn't the man she believed him to be—he had a mean streak and fast right hook. And she'd never seen it coming.

The day wore on, hours slowly rolling past, and they pressed the cattle the limit. They could slow down tomorrow and allow for more rests, but today they needed to cover ground so they could get to the camp. They were all hungry, and Dakota was starting to feel a little light-headed. A day of riding and herding was tough with no food in your stomach, and while they were all used to pushing themselves, they also knew their limits. The camp would be a very welcome sight.

"Penny for your thoughts?"

She turned to see Harley approaching and she smiled wistfully. "Nothing."

The cattle were moving easily enough and, as they rode, the day warmed. Harley pulled off his jacket, and she caught sight of that crudely drawn tattoo on his forearm once more.

"What is that?" she asked.

"A cross."

"Yeah, I see that," she said with a short laugh. "Where did you get it?" Harley didn't look inclined to answer so she added, "Word around here is that you've spent some time in prison."

Harley cut her a cautious look then sighed. "So much for keeping a low profile. Who told you—Elliot?"

She nodded. "Sort of. He told Andy. Andy told me."

"You two are closer than you like to let on," Harley said with a wry smile.

"Me and Elliot?" she asked.

He laughed and shook his head. "Nice try. You know who I'm talking about. You and the boss. There's something there."

"We have a bit of history," she said. "But it's nothing more than that."

Or perhaps a little more than that. In fact, there seemed to be parts of their history she hadn't even known until today. Andy hid his heart well, but deep underneath it all, he cared more than she'd ever known.

"What kind of history?" he asked.

"It's personal."

"More personal that my prison time?" he quipped, and when she glanced over at him she caught Harley's boyish grin. These last four days without shaving didn't seem to make any difference for him.

"We ran in the same circles in high school," she said. "Nothing terribly interesting."

Harley let out a shrill whistle and he touched a cow's flank with a long twig. It picked up its pace. Harley had admitted to having spent time in prison, and she was still balancing that out in her head. She'd half expected him to deny it, to point out that Elliot couldn't stand him, and a part of her would have been happier with that outcome. Elliot was easier to dislike—at least for her. Couldn't something go back to being black and white?

"So what did you do to go to prison?" she asked.

Harley chewed on one side of cheek then he sighed. "I was a cattle rustler."

His words took a moment to sink in and, when

they did, she stared at him, aghast. Not only did he
look about fourteen years old, but he had applied for
work as a drover. If he'd been imprisoned for stealing cattle, he had no business working this kind of
job ever again.

"You shouldn't be working here, then," she said
shortly.

"It's the only work I know," he said. "What am I
supposed to do? I'm not qualified for anything else."

"Be a short-order cook," she said. "I don't really
care. If you've been busted for cattle rustling, this
kind of job would be a big temptation."

Harley's cheeks colored and he looked away. Was
he embarrassed?

"Look, I was a kid. I got involved with the wrong
guys, and I can't blame a troubled home or anything
like that. I thought they were cool because they were
tough and dangerous, and I was bored with the Sunday-
school humdrum at home. But when my new friends
needed a fall guy, guess who went to prison?"

"And the tattoo?" she asked.

"My cellmate did it for me. It has—" He looked
away, out across the plains. "It has personal signifi-
cance."

She nodded. Fair enough, but she still didn't think
he belonged there. He was all Billy the Kid in appearances, cherubic face and Bible in his pocket. Most
of the cattle losses were inside jobs these days, and
Dakota took this kind of thing very personally. The
Masons had lost about fifty head one year due to a
shady ranch hand, and that kind of loss hit a rancher

where it hurt. There wasn't a huge profit margin in this kind of work.

"I'm not the same guy," Harley said, his hand moving up toward the New Testament in his pocket. "I've learned from my mistakes. Sunday school isn't so bad, after all."

Harley was a likeable kid, but she knew better than to trust based on charisma. She might have missed the subtleties going on between Andy and Dwight, but that didn't make her blind. If a girl sat back on her haunches and kept her eyes open, she could learn a whole lot.

"There was this woman in Hope," Dakota said after a moment. "She had a reputation around town as being pretty loose. She'd slept with every available man, and a few of the unavailable ones, too. Then one day she went to church and the church members were so happy to see that she'd come looking for some answers and some faith. She got involved with all the church activities. She helped out with Sunday school and baked pies for the bake sale… Then one day, they found out that she'd been sleeping with the head elder. The *married* head elder."

Harley winced. "What happened?"

"Well, the church was rocked. I mean, this man was a community pillar. His wife left him and they got divorced. It was very messy. He and his wife had three sons together, and those boys never forgave him. The woman with the reputation ended up marrying the head elder and they moved away. Don't know where they are now, or if they even lasted.

The ex-wife still attends that church, though. As do the boys."

Harley was silent for a moment. "That's too bad."

"It is," she said. "And the moral of that story is that sometimes people show an interest in religion for their own selfish reasons."

"Are you suggesting something?" Harley asked, caution entering his tone.

Dakota knew why she was angry—she'd really liked Harley. And if he betrayed them, if he was up to no good, after all, it would hurt more than the Granger profit line. Somehow she needed a bit of redemption out of this whole cattle drive—she needed it to be about something more than the feelings she and Andy could never act on.

"Are you really trying to live a better life?" she asked after a moment.

"Yes." His tone was honest and quiet. "I'm here to make a little bit of money the honest way so that I can stay long enough to talk to my sister, and then I'm going home. Simple as that."

"Okay," she said. "I've had men lie to my face before, and they've been as sweet-looking as you are. Don't be one of them."

"No, ma'am." Harley tipped his hat.

She sincerely wished him the best, but if he came around the Mason ranch looking for work, he'd be stark out of luck.

BOB GRANGER RODE out to meet them when the sun was high. He led a packhorse behind him loaded with supplies, and they watched him approach for two hours before they finally met. He crept over the golden, rolling hills, a tiny figure with a tiny shadow, moving steadily up toward the foothills. Provisions were coming, and Andy was relieved.

Personally he could have dealt with a full day without food. It wouldn't have been comfortable or his first choice, but his relief at seeing that pack-horse had less to do with his own hunger and more to do with Dakota.

She'd been getting steadily paler as the morning wore on. She was tough as leather, that woman, and she put in just as much work as he'd ever done. She'd be the last to admit to weakening, but she was hungry, and the old protective instinct kicked in. She was driving the Granger cattle, and she deserved to do that on a full stomach.

When they finally met up with Bob at noon, they all dismounted and he pulled out the food he'd brought—roast beef sandwiches, chocolate bars for energy, and dried fruit. Andy passed the first sandwich to Dakota and she didn't wait on niceties, tearing open the waxed paper and taking a big, jaw-cracking bite. Andy couldn't help the grin that came to his face.

"Last we ate was what we could scrape from the bottom of our saddlebags last night," Andy said, tossing the next sandwich to Harley and then taking one himself.

"Should have crossed with the rest," Bob said disapprovingly.

"We would have lost calves," Andy replied. Was

his uncle really questioning a leadership decision in front of the drovers?

"Might have lost more than calves if I didn't come out to fetch you," Bob retorted.

"I'm fully capable of getting the cattle home," Andy said. "And coming out to bring supplies is called teamwork, Bob."

"Is that what we are?" his uncle asked wryly. "A team?"

The words were loaded. Andy had relinquished any right to call on family solidarity when he'd sold his land to the highest bidder against the family's wishes. He didn't only need to prove himself to the hired help, he needed to prove himself to his own kin. They were all waiting for him to fail—for some sort of karmic retribution to even the score.

"The river was too swollen to get the calves across," Andy said. "So we went downstream. We crossed this morning."

"Ah." Bob nodded slowly. "Lose any?"

"Not one." He'd made the right call. He knew that beyond the shadow of a doubt. And he hadn't made the decision alone—Dakota had been a big part of it. Bob would have disagreed with him no matter what he'd chosen.

"Eat up." That was as close to an atta-boy as Andy was going to get out of his uncle. Uncle Bob was Andy's late father's brother, and he saw things in a very linear way. There was family, there was land and there was cattle. And then there were the idiots who messed things up for the serious ranchers. Andy fell into the latter category.

They ate the food Bob had brought and, before half an hour had passed, they all remounted and started back toward camp.

"Elliot had a few things to say about Harley, there," Bob said, lowering his voice.

"Harley had a few things to say about Elliot, too," Andy replied with a grim smile. "Harley's leaving when the drive is done. It'll take care of itself."

"If Chet had been here, he'd—"

"Yeah, well, Chet wasn't," Andy interrupted. "And I'm here because Chet wanted me here. Let me do my job."

Andy was tired of defending himself to this blasted family. They disagreed with him. They were embarrassed of him. He was a mark on their good name. Fine. But this was emotional for them, and there came a point when Andy got good and tired of wading through everyone else's emotions. If they hated him, so be it. He'd be out of their hair in a few days and they could all settle into some nice, comfortable resentment and stew to their hearts' content.

Bob grunted but didn't say anything further. Riding was easier with a full belly, and Andy found his eyes straying toward Dakota more often than he'd care to have his uncle notice. She rode ahead of Andy, chestnut ponytail bouncing on her back, hat pushed back and one hand resting on her thigh. Her hips pivoted easily with the movement of the big horse beneath her, and when she looked out over the ever-flattening hills, he caught her face in profile.

Was she ever beautiful.

He'd always known it, but riding with her on the open countryside somehow made her more vibrant, more alive. The fact that they were now on their way back to the ranch also made this time with her all the more precious. If there was a way to make it last, he'd do pretty much anything, but there were too many things out of his control. If it were just about him and Dakota, maybe a few those barriers would have been surmountable, but it wasn't. It never was about two people. Everyone had a whole host of others attached to them, people who refused to be discounted. Family didn't just wish you well and wave goodbye. There were always strings, obligations. And sometimes the mistakes you made couldn't be atoned for, after all.

When they arrived at the camp that evening, Lydia had a meal of smoked sausages, coal-baked potatoes and creamed corn. Andy tried not to be obvious about it, but his gaze kept trailing back toward Dakota. She sat on a chunk of wood, her plate balanced on her knees, and he realized that even with greasy fingers and a little dab of ketchup in one corner of her mouth, she was still the most beautiful woman he'd ever met.

She caught him watching once or twice, and a small smile flickered at her lips. She felt it, too. He knew that she did, but they were one day away from civilization—close enough to Hope that their phones would pick up reception again once they turned them back on.

Bob and Lydia were eating now that everyone else had been served, and Andy felt a pang of sadness looking at his aunt and uncle. They'd weathered over the years, grayed, plumped, but he still remembered the old days when he'd go apple picking at their orchard, or the year his uncle broke his leg and it was Andy's job to cut their grass on the riding lawnmower. He'd hated doing it—for free, no less—but he'd felt proud of himself all the same in that boyish emotional conflict that meant a valuable lesson was being learned.

Bob might not have a whole lot of respect left for him, but Andy hadn't forgotten where he came from. Not completely.

The low hum of voices mingled with the creak of tree limbs as the wind moved the towering evergreen boughs above their heads. The trees broke most of the cold wind, but the air was still frigid, making the fire a welcome comfort. Elliot and Harley stood away from the group, out by the edge of the trees, and what must have started as a private conversation now missed that mark by a mile.

"Everyone knows about your history." Elliot's voice carried, and Andy's attention snapped toward the lanky cowboy.

"I don't really care," Harley said. "I'm not here to make myself look better than I am. I'm here for my sister."

"I don't have her." Elliot's tone dripped sarcasm.

"Have I carried her in my pocket? You're here for me. You want to make sure that everyone hates me as much as you do before you're done."

Andy and Dakota exchanged a look. Apparently the two drovers were going to sort out their business right here, right now. It might be just as well if they could manage it civilly, enough. The tension had been thrumming for days.

"I don't hate you." Harley's voice stayed controlled. "I just don't think you're good enough for my sister."

Elliot barked out a laugh. "So why come to me about that? What is this, an arrangement between men? Are we bartering her off? She's a free woman, and she can do what she likes."

"Just to be clear—" Harley's control was starting to waver "—you got her pregnant, you brought her to Montana to live with you, you intend to keep this arrangement going, but you won't give her the one thing she wants most right now?"

"How do you know what she wants most?" Elliot demanded. "You came to our door and she wouldn't even open it. Take a hint."

"Because I know *her*!" Harley's voice rose. "You sleep with her for a couple of months and you think that's knowing someone? There is a family heirloom wedding dress in my mother's closet. Do you know about that? Did you know that Holly tried that dress on just last year? When she turned eighteen, my father gave her a string of pearls and he told her that he wanted her to wear them before her wedding day so that she'd remember what she was worth. She cried when she put those pearls on, and she wore them every week to church. But when she left home to come to Montana to live with you, she left those pearls behind."

Dakota paled slightly at those words and put her plate down on the ground at her feet, turning toward Harley and Elliot, a frown creasing her forehead.

"Maybe she's changed her mind about a few things." Elliot turned away then stomped back. He seemed to have forgotten the rest of them watching. "Ever think of that? Ever think that maybe she thinks for herself now, and maybe she doesn't want the weight of all those expectations on her?"

"And maybe you convinced her that she wasn't worth those pearls anymore," Harley snapped. "Maybe you convinced her that she wasn't worth commitment, her great-grandmother's wedding dress or a man willing to promise his life to her!"

Elliot's face paled and his lips quivered with fury. "I will not—" He paused, putting obvious effort into controlling himself "I will *never* be backed into a shotgun wedding!"

"I know." Harley's face twisted into a cold smile. "And I'm glad of that. I just want her to see it for herself."

Elliot grabbed Harley by the collar and dragged him forward.

This had gone far enough. Andy crossed the camp in several strides and grabbed Elliot's finger, bending it backward painfully until he released the younger man.

"Enough!" Andy roared.

"For all your sense of honor, Harley—" Elliot spat "—your sister is embarrassed of you. If you care about her at all, you'll walk away and let her forget that her own brother is an ex-con. You think I'm disgracing her? I'm not the one who humiliated the entire family by cattle rustling! I did her a favor by keeping my mouth shut about you!"

Cattle rustling? Andy stared at Harley in shock. Was that what had sent the kid to prison?

"Enough!" Andy repeated, his voice vibrating with repressed anger. "Leave each other alone. You can work this out on your own time—not here!"

"Speaking of family disgraces..." Elliot sneered. "You might be running this drive, but no one's forgotten what you've done, either, Granger."

Elliot jerked his arm out of Andy's grip and stalked back to the fire. The rest of the drovers sat in awkward silence, turning their attention to their food again. Harley stayed put, turned his back on all of them and stared out at the lengthening shadows across the plains as the sun sank.

Andy went back to the fire, attempting to keep his expression neutral. He wouldn't be chased off by the likes of Elliot with a few snide comments. Elliot was hired help, and Andy was there representing the family, whether the blasted family wanted him or not. There were some things he didn't like to advertise, like when a drover's snarky remarks hit too close to home.

Bob looked up and met Andy's gaze for the first

time since they'd returned to camp. The firelight flickered across his features and he cradled a tin mug of coffee between his roughened hands. He didn't say a word, but Andy could read it all in that weather-beaten face.

Elliot's words had hit the mark—no one was going to forget.

Chapter Eleven

The next morning Dakota awoke before sunrise. The sky was still dark and when she fumbled with her watch in the cocoon of her sleeping bag, she saw it was only four. She wasn't going to go back to sleep, though. She normally woke up close to this time at home for chores, and convincing her body to do anything else would be more work than simply getting up.

The ground was cold and hard, and as she moved around pulling on clothes and running a brush through her hair, a heaviness clung to her. She'd hoped it would've disappeared during the night, but it hadn't.

She and Andy had been careful all evening—polite nods, few words, a cautious distance when they sat next to each other. They were no longer alone, and she could feel the difference that meant between them. Alone— or relatively so with only Harley for company—they were freer with each other, they'd naturally lean toward each other in the glow of the fire.

But last night they'd both been rigid, trying not

to lean together lest people see them and think there was something going on between them.

Which wouldn't be wrong.

That was the thing—there *was* something between them. They could pretend otherwise, but it didn't change the truth. She'd been developing feelings for Andy, and she could see it in his eyes that he felt the same. But the people around them, the pressures, the expectations, all changed things. They weren't free to feel anything.

As Dakota came out of her tent, she could still hear the snores of the other drovers. Apparently a hard, cold ground didn't interrupt their slumber at all and she crept away from the tents, wanting some time to herself in the dimness of predawn.

Dakota did up her jacket and slipped to the edge of camp. Outside the shelter of the trees the wind was sharp with cold. Snowflakes danced in the air as the edge of the horizon glowed the deepest of mauves. A horse plodded toward her and she recognized Andy immediately. He'd been on the last patrol of the night—she should have remembered. He reined in Romeo and dismounted, all without saying a word.

"Morning," she said softly.

"First one up?" His voice was gravelly and quiet.

She nodded. She wouldn't be for long. Soon someone else would awake, make some noise, and the rest would start pulling their things together…but not yet. Right now, in these dusky moments before dawn, they were the only ones.

"Walk with me," he said, holding out his hand, and his gesture sent a flood of relief through her. From all their careful distance last night, that outstretched hand closed the gap again. She took his hand and they walked briskly away from camp.

"We'll be home by supper," Andy said. His hand was warm, enveloping hers in comforting strength.

"It's not going to be the same," she said.

"Never is," he agreed. "Home changes everything."

Normally that would be a good thing, but not this time. Home wasn't a welcome bastion of warmth and food, it was the finish line—the goodbye. He pulled her in closer and wrapped his arms around her waist, his mouth so close she could feel his breath against her lips. Still, he didn't close the distance, his mouth hovering.

"Andy..." she whispered.

"I'm going to miss this," he murmured, and then his warm lips came down on hers, soft and tender, then growing more insistent as he pulled her closer still.

Her heart sped up and she wanted to be closer to him, away from bulky coats and prying eyes. She wanted to feel his heart against hers and rest her cheek against his neck... She wanted kisses that didn't stop.

But she pulled back—they did have to stop this. Tempting as he was, why should she torment herself with something that could never be?

"I know your parents are going to hate me for a long time," Andy said huskily. "But maybe you could point out that I'm not the devil...you know, if it ever comes up?"

He reached down and wiped a bit of moisture from her lip with the pad of his thumb. He smiled teasingly, but it didn't cover the sadness that glistened in those green eyes.

"I could try," she said with a low laugh. "I'm not sure what good it would do."

"Yeah, I know..." He stopped and pulled her around to face him. "Dakota, what if it didn't have to end just because the drive did?"

"How?" she asked, shaking her head. "We can't just ride off into the sunset, Andy. That's not real life."

"But we could ride off to Billings." He caught her gaze and dipped his head to keep the eye contact. "I'm serious, Dakota. I know this is nuts, but I'm actually pretty well off. I've got a house, a business, friends... Come back with me. We could make a life together—"

The life, the home, the promises... If anything had illuminated the fallacy of those possibilities, it was Harley's sister and Elliot. They might avoid a painful goodbye, but for what? The drawn-out pain of a relationship that didn't have what it took to last in real life, with real families?

"What about my family?" she asked.

"We could make some money in Billings— enough to buy some more land—and come back. We could figure it out," he said. "Together." And while the offer was tempting, it lacked too many things she needed in her life: the land, her family ranch, the community of Hope that she'd grown up in. It lacked *people*, the very people who had loved her, raised her, defended her when Dwight got abusive and who were a part of her deepest core. Could she just walk away from her parents? They'd be heart-broken. Brody would be furious and God help Andy if her brother got his hands on him.

"No." She pulled out of his arms. It was too hard to think with him this close. "You're offering what Elliot offered Holly, and that doesn't work. I have a family, and I can't just walk away from them. I can't be happy that way! And the truth is, they aren't going to just forgive you and or see what I see in you—"

"Which is?" he pressed.

Tears misted her eyes. "I see the guy who told Dwight to be good to me…the guy who came back to run a cattle drive knowing that everyone would hate him… You're a good man, Andy. I know that, but the rest of the town isn't so convinced."

Andy held her gaze for a moment then looked away. "I know."

"And I'm sorry." Why did this have to be so hard? They'd known it was impossible from the beginning. That was why they'd done their best not to feel this way—to nip it in the bud. "But what if…"

Dakota was almost afraid to say it. Running off to Billings couldn't answer their problems, but what if Andy didn't have to leave right away? What if they could put this goodbye off somehow and get more time to think.

"What if what?" he asked softly.

"What if you stayed?"

Andy sucked in a deep breath then released a slow sigh. "I don't belong here, Dakota. You have your family, parents who are still around, a whole community that has your best interest at heart, but I don't. They hate me here, and that's not about to change. My own uncle can barely stand to look at me. I came to do my brother a favor, and that's it. I can't stay."

And she'd known that, too. Nothing had actually changed over the last few days, except for their feelings for each other.

"Don't you see?" Anger was replacing the sadness now—something easier to deal with, something she could wield. "We've been talking about Harley's sister this whole time, and deep down I've thought she was a little bit dumb. I mean, I'll defend a woman's right to choose her own future until I go blue in the face, but deep down I thought she was blind not to see it!"

"See what?" Andy's eyes clouded. "You think I'm no better than Elliot?"

"Yes!" She dashed a tear off of her cheek with the back of her hand. "It's the same situation, don't you see? They wanted to be together, but they didn't think it through. You're offering a life in Billings, but it's no more than Elliot offered—"

"That's not true," Andy growled, anger flashing back at her in those green eyes. "I'm not offering to share rent, Dakota. I'm offering me, all of me. I'm offering to get married!"

Dakota felt like the breath was knocked out of her

and she stared at Andy in surprise. He was asking her to marry him? Did that change things? It made her heart leap, and it made her wish for things so hard that it ached inside her very core, but did it truly change anything?

"You're offering all the right things, Andy," she said, her voice choking with tears. "But you're forgetting something. A wedding isn't about just you and me—"

"It should be," he said.

She shook her head. "Those pews would be empty, and that would break my heart. I can't give up my entire family, Andy."

Andy nodded, and his eyes misted, too. "I know, gorgeous," he whispered. "I love you, and I could never ask it of you."

The horizon was pink now and the sky brightened ever so slowly, illuminating the forms of lounging cows chewing their cud. If only things could stay as simple as they were out here...

"You love me?" she asked softly.

"Would I ask you to marry me if I didn't?" He reached out to move a hair away from her eyes. "Not that it matters, I guess."

Dakota took a step back, out of his reach. If he touched her again, she'd only move back into his strong arms, and no matter how long she put this off, it wouldn't change anything.

Behind them, a pot clanked, and Dakota turned to see Lydia standing at the tree line looking at them.

They'd been seen, and Lydia was making as much noise as possible to warn them.

"We have cattle to move," Dakota said quickly. She met his eyes once more, but she knew better than to take even one step toward him. His eyes held a silent request that she couldn't answer and so she did the only thing left—turned back toward camp. With every step, her heart ached more, but she wouldn't make Holly's mistake. A woman might need love, but she also needed family, and one could never make up for the other.

THAT DAY THE ride was smooth. Everyone was looking forward to getting back, and the cattle perked up, remembering the warmth of home and hay. He and Dakota didn't talk much. They stayed busy keeping the cattle moving, and truthfully, it looked like she was avoiding him. Maybe that was for the best. He couldn't change her family's opinion of him so easily, and he couldn't take back the land sale that ruined the Masons' property. He couldn't give her the whole package—a loving husband who melded well with her own family. He could love her, he could be faithful and devoted, but he had no control over the rest. And she deserved to have the whole package.

When they finally got back to the ranch, the sun was sinking at their backs. They unsaddled the horses and gave them all a much deserved rubdown. And when Andy had thanked the drovers for their service and promised paychecks for the next morning, everyone went their own way.

Except Dakota. She stood there in front of the barn, her face glowing in the last of the sunset.

"I'm going to miss you," she said.

"This isn't goodbye," he said. "I still have to give you your paycheck tomorrow."

"I know." She pulled the elastic out of her hair and let it fall loose around her shoulders. It changed the look of her—softened her—and all he wanted was to push his fingers into that hair and pull her into his arms, but he wouldn't. They knew where things stood. But he had other business to take care of—business connected to her, but not entirely about her, either. Dwight had been his friend, and he wasn't about to just walk away from what he'd done to Dakota. "You said Dwight spends a lot of time in the bar," Andy said after a moment.

She nodded. "Unless he's changed overnight."

"The Honky Tonk?" he clarified.

She nodded again but looked at him dubiously. "Why do you ask?"

"I told you before," he said with a shrug. "I have a bone to pick with him."

"Andy, let it go." Her eyes flashed annoyance. "It was a long time ago and I don't feel like dragging it up again. I've moved on. You should, too."

"Hey." Andy caught her eye and held it. "He was my best friend, okay? I'm not dragging you into anything. This is between me and Dwight."

She shook her head. "I'm not yours to protect, Andy."

"And I'm not yours to stop," he retorted.

A couple of beats of silence passed between them and color rose in her cheeks. She nodded a couple of times, swallowed, then said, "Okay. Fine. I'll leave you to it, then. But don't do anything stupid and get yourself arrested."

Was she worried about him?

"Scout's honor."

Dakota turned and walked away. She didn't turn back. She got into her truck and he watched as her tires spun up some gravel and she drove off. He had no idea what she was feeling, or if it was anywhere as aching as what he felt. Soon enough he'd be driving out of Hope for good, too, and he'd have to nurse his torn heart in Billings. Dakota would move on, of course. She'd find a good guy and settle down to have a few kids and run a ranch, and the man who ended up with her would be a lucky son of a gun.

Finding a woman who made him feel the way Dakota did wouldn't be easy. In his thirty years he'd never found one to match her.

Half an hour later Andy pulled his truck into an empty space in front of the Honky Tonk Bar. It was a seedy-looking place, squat and small with blackened windows. No one wanted to be reminded of the time of day or night when drinking their worries away.

The *T* in the neon sign flickered. When he opened the door, he was met with stuffy, beer-scented air, the jangly, old-fashioned country music from the juke box and the jumble of laughter and voices.

He scanned the crowd—it was still pretty early, but the bar was obviously doing good business. In a far corner a few cowboys sat around a table, nursing bottles. There was another table close to them filled with women in their mid-forties, laughing and joking. A couple danced on the floor, swaying off-rhythm to the music, oblivious to anyone else around them.

At the bar sat a solitary figure, shoulders hunched. Andy hadn't seen Dwight in a few years. He'd heard that he'd gone to seed, but they hadn't actually crossed paths, so staring at the back of this fellow, Andy wasn't sure if he was looking at the right man or not. If this was Dwight, he had no idea what he was even going to say to him. He'd gone over a few different options in his head on the way over, but he still had no clue which words would come out of his mouth. He just knew that he couldn't leave this.

Dakota might not be his to protect, but that didn't just turn off his feelings. But this wasn't one hundred percent about Dakota, either. If it had been a different woman that Dwight had beaten, Andy would still be here—beating on a woman couldn't be just left alone.

As if on cue, the man turned and glanced over his shoulder. He was older, more worn, but it was Dwight Peterson, all right. He saw Andy, and didn't seem to recognize him at first, then froze.

Andy crossed the bar and dropped onto the stool next to Dwight. His blond hair was tousled and greasy. He clutched a glass of whiskey with a white-knuckled grip and shot Andy a sidelong glance.

"Look who's back," Dwight said.

"For a few days, at least," Andy said. "Long time, Dwight."

"Yup." Dwight drained the glass and put it back on the counter with a thunk. "So what do you want?"

Andy shrugged. "We used to be friends."

"Used to be." Dwight snorted. "Then you got your fancy life in Billings and didn't have time for the rest of us. So, what, you back slumming it for a few days?"

He'd gotten an education and then gotten a job. What was he supposed to do, sit around in Hope while his brother ran the ranch?

"I got a job, man," Andy retorted. "You resent me for that? How have you been?"

"Hard to get work around here," Dwight said.

"It would be when you're soused."

Dwight didn't answer that and Andy didn't expect him to. There was plenty of ranch work to be had around here if you were able-bodied and willing to work hard. Being sober would also be an asset, but from what Andy could tell, Dwight already had a bad reputation, and that was both pathetic and sad. He didn't have to turn out like this.

"Where are you living these days?" Andy asked after a moment.

"With my mom. She needs me to help out around the place…"

Andy seriously doubted he was living with his mom because the old lady needed him so badly. Likely, Mrs. Peterson would be good and glad to have her son out from under her roof, but Dwight drank away what little money he got his hands on. He had a problem—a big one. Dwight had turned out a little bit too much like his old man.

"I saw Dakota," Andy said.

Dwight nodded slowly then raised two fingers at the bartender. Andy shook his head in the negative when the bartender looked to Andy for his order. He wasn't here to drink. A filled glass slid down the counter toward them and Dwight picked it up and took a sip. Andy let his words hang in the air a little longer, but Dwight didn't open his mouth.

"You have nothing to say?" Andy asked icily.

"How's she doing?" Dwight asked at last.

How was she? She was just as amazing as she'd always been, except there was a crack in her now—a place where Dwight had broken her faith in men and she'd never quite healed.

"She told me about how you used to smack her around."

Dwight's hand trembled and he put the drink down. "That was a long time ago."

Anger coursed through Andy's veins until his entire body pulsed with it. It might have been a long time ago in Dwight's estimation, but he'd seen the way Dakota reacted with Elliot on the cattle drive, and it wasn't far enough in her past yet.

"You remember when you started dating her?" Andy asked, keeping his voice low.

Dwight shrugged. "What about it?"

"I backed off," Andy snapped. "You said you were in love with her, that you'd marry her—"

"She broke it off!" Dwight snapped. "I *would* have married her!"

This wasn't about broken engagements, this was about broken promises. Andy stared hard at the counter, attempting to keep that simmering anger under control. "You said you'd take care of her, man. Then you started hitting her."

"That was only—"

"When you drank." Andy smiled icily. "I know."

"It only happened a couple of times."

"Three times, she said. That's three times too many."

"So what are you here for?" Dwight asked, looking over at Andy warily. He only met Andy's eye for a second before he dropped his gaze like a kicked dog. He looked like he was expecting a punch, but Andy wasn't even sure Dwight would defend himself if he did. Back in the truck, Andy had fantasized about a few different scenarios that ended in him punching Dwight square in the face, but now that he was staring at him, Andy didn't have it in him anymore.

Dwight's face had scars from fights, and Andy had a feeling that Dwight knew exactly what it felt like to be beaten up. Andy didn't need to educate him in that. But under those scars, under the smell of booze that seemed to emanate from every pore of the man's body, was the shadow of the old Dwight Peterson that Andy used to know—the buddy through thick and thin.

"I've gotta tell you, Dwight, I wanted to give you a taste of what you did to her," Andy said quietly.

Dwight was silent. He shifted on the stool, looking ready to raise an arm in self-defense, but there wasn't any pride left. Just shame and booze.

"I've got a better idea." Andy pulled out a few bills and put them on the counter to cover Dwight's bill. "Come on."

"What?" Dwight snapped. "Where?"

"You can sit here and drink the night away," Andy said, hooking him under the arm. "Or you can come out with me."

"I thought you hated me," Dwight said.

"I still might," Andy retorted. "But you're safer with me than you are in here. Let's go."

Dwight took a moment to consider and then got shakily to his feet. "What about giving me a job at your swanky car dealership in Billings?"

"Nope." Andy led the way through the bar to the front door. "I don't hire drunks."

"So where're we going?" Dwight asked, rubbing a hand across his nose.

They stepped outside into the autumn cold and Dwight shivered.

"For a fresh start, buddy," Andy said gruffly. "There's an Alcoholics Anonymous meeting happening in the basement of the Good Shepherd church in—" he looked at his watch "—fifteen minutes." He lifted up his phone as proof, the website open on the screen.

"I don't need a support group," Dwight sneered, and he took a step back toward the bar.

"Dwight, you hit her!" Andy's voice rang out clear and sharp, and Dwight deflated once more. Andy hooked a thumb toward his truck. "I'll drive you down. I'll sit in the meeting with you."

Dwight stood in the flickering light of the neon sign, the *T* buzzing softly every time it flashed. He looked sad, worn out, empty.

"Why are you doing this?" he asked after a moment.

"Because we used to be friends," Andy said.

"Not friends now?" Dwight asked hopefully.

Was Dwight his friend? No, Andy couldn't lie and say that he was. He couldn't be the buddy of the man who'd terrorized a woman like that, especially Dakota. But Dwight wasn't a threat to Dakota anymore. He was a broken man, and Dakota was well free of him. Dwight looked at him hopefully. He was half drunk, which might account for this sudden burst of neediness, and Andy sighed.

"You've got to pull yourself together, man," Andy said at last. "You need to go to these meetings every week. You need a sponsor. You've got to work the steps. You can be better than this."

Andy opened the passenger-side door and gestured for Dwight to get in. No, Dwight wasn't his friend anymore, but for the memory of a friendship that used to mean a lot to both of them, Andy was willing to do this. Deep down under the addiction there was a guy who used to be his buddy.

"But let me be clear," Andy said as Dwight got in. "You need to stay away from Dakota. For good."

Dwight didn't answer and Andy banged the door shut before heading around to the driver's side. If Andy ever heard that Dwight had raised his hand to Dakota again, his good will would be spent and he'd come back down here and follow his previous instinct to beat the ever-loving tar out of him.

Chapter Twelve

Dakota expected to drop into bed that night, exhausted from the drive, but instead she found herself lying awake. Granted, she'd gone to bed early, but it hadn't been just any cattle drive this year and coming home to her own bed didn't provide the closure it usually did. Sure, the cattle were back. Her job was done. But she'd fallen in love with the wrong man despite her best efforts not to.

Her bedroom was the same room she'd slept in since she was a child. It had changed over the years and the toys and childish knickknacks were down in the basement now. It was a sparse bedroom— white walls, a bed with several quilts on top. She had a standing wardrobe in one corner, a writing desk in the other, and a hand-made rag rug that she and Grandma Mason had sewn together years ago. A bookcase held some framed black-and-white photos of grandparents and great-grandparents, a few awards and three shelves packed tight with her favorite books.

How long should she stay in her parents' house?

She'd planned on moving out a few years earlier, but then the ranch had started to dry up and the workload had increased drastically. So she'd stuck around. Besides, her parents couldn't afford to hire another worker to replace her right now, and she had as much at stake in this land as they did. So she stayed on, keeping watch over her hopeful inheritance. This land wasn't just the family ranch, it was her future, and she was willing to sacrifice certain things to see her dreams of running it become a reality.

Now she lay in bed, staring at the shadows the moonlight and tree branches made on her ceiling. Tears welled in her eyes. She'd hoped it would all feel differently once she was home again, that her feelings for Andy would fade and she'd see clearly that it was an impossibility. And while she did recognize that a relationship would never work, her feelings hadn't faded. If anything, she felt her loss all the more sharply. It stabbed deeper than she'd thought possible, deeper than even calling off her wedding had wounded her. How had this happened in such a short period of time?

"I fell in love with Andy Granger..." Whispering the words aloud wasn't as jarring as she'd hoped it'd be. Probably because it was true. She'd seen a side to Andy on that cattle drive that she'd never seen before, and when she'd looked into his eyes and felt those strong arms wrap around her, she'd known what she was giving up. In her mind's eye she could see what a life with Andy would be like—waking up in those arms each morning, starting a family, getting older... But the one thing she couldn't picture was doing all of that in Billings. And that's why it was so impossible. She couldn't just walk away from this land, and yet she couldn't tear herself completely free of Andy, either.

Downstairs the phone rang twice and then was picked up. She could hear the muffled sound of her father's voice, but couldn't make out the words. She wiped the tears from her cheeks and sat up in bed. This was no use.

She looked at her cell phone, tempted to dial Andy's number, but she didn't want to wake him up to say... what exactly? That she missed him? That her heart physically ached right now because of what she was walking away from? They'd already said it all...the only problem was that home wasn't dulling the pain for her like it was supposed to do. Coming home hadn't changed a thing.

Dakota grabbed her bathrobe and shoved her feet into her slippers. She'd go downstairs and get a bowl of ice cream or something. She ambled out of her room and started down the stairs. Her father was coming up, still dressed in jeans and a red, flannel shirt, rolled up to his elbows like he'd always worn his shirts. She stopped short when she saw his face. He was ashen.

"Dad?" Dakota put a hand out. "What happened?"

He blinked twice before he said anything and when he spoke, his voice was raspy. "I just got a call from your brother's unit commander—" He swallowed hard. "Brody's been injured...badly, they say. A land mine went off and—" Her father's voice shook. "He's in surgery right now. They don't know how long he'll be there, but he'll be sent home once he's stable enough for transport."

His words took a moment to sink in and Dakota stared at her father in shock. The worst had happened. They'd told each other that the worst couldn't happen, wouldn't happen, because of the very fact it was the worst-case scenario. They were somehow protected from it all because they'd laughed at it, refused to give it root. But Brody had been wounded—their fears had come true—and she could only pray he'd survive.

A land mine… Tears welled up in her eyes.

"Is he going to die, Dad?"

"They don't think so," her father said, sucking in a wavering breath. "But his combat days are likely over. They say his leg is in bad shape. They'll call again once he's out of surgery and give us an update."

She nodded numbly. "Okay, so that's good news, then. It could have been worse."

Her father raked a hand through his sparse hair. This was what they had been trying to protect Brody from by keeping their secret, and it had befallen him anyway. Was her father thinking the same thing?

"When he left, I was so angry," her father said. "They say not to go to bed angry with your wife, but I think it's worse to let your child leave when you're mad like that…"

"He knows you love him, Dad," Dakota said. "You two just never really saw eye to eye—"

"I just want him home safe." Her father's chin trembled. "To me, he's still my boy who wanted shoulder rides. And I want him back home in one piece…or as close to it as the surgeons can manage."

Dakota sank onto the stairs and her father sat next to her. They were both quiet for a few moments then her father patted her knee with his gnarled hand.

"Dakota, do I put too much pressure on you?" he asked quietly.

"No."

What was too much pressure? He let her be a part of running the family land, and that came with pressure that she was gladly willing to shoulder. She was a grown woman now and didn't need to be sheltered from the hard things in life.

"Well, I'm going to tell you what I should have told your brother before he left," her father said gruffly. "I want you to be happy. That's it. You make your choices and live your life, and if you end up happy, I'll have done my job well."

Dakota leaned over and put her head on her father's shoulder. "But I am happy, Dad."

The words were hollow because she was furthest thing from happy right now. But that wasn't her father's fault. He didn't even suspect what had happened between her and Andy.

"Are you? Living here with us?" Her father smiled sadly. "Follow your heart, Dakota. I won't give you grief."

Perhaps she didn't look as happy as she claimed to be. She couldn't say that life had been easy with

Dwight's abuse, a canceled wedding and the land drying up before their eyes. But happiness didn't necessarily come with an easy life, and she wasn't one to back down from the challenges. Right now, the ache inside her wasn't because of Dwight or the land, it was because of Andy. And she'd have to deal with this particular heartbreak alone.

He'd said he loved her…he'd asked her to marry him and move to Billings…

And Brody was wounded and would be on his way home as soon as they could safely transport him. Why did everything have to knot together into one unmanageable tangle?

Her father pushed himself to his feet. "I'm going to go and wake up your mother."

He walked heavily up the stairs and paused at the master bedroom door. He hung his head for a moment, as if steeling himself, then turned the knob. She heard her mother's groggy voice. "What time is it?"

Follow her heart… Did her father have any idea of where her heart led? Because right now, with every beat, it was yearning for the man who had decimated their property.

She bowed her head, meaning to say a prayer for her brother's recovery, but instead of a whispered prayer, she only met with tears. Her heart was breaking—for the man she'd fallen in love with against her better judgment, for her brother, who was wounded in the line of duty, still so far from home, and for her father, who had loved so hard but forgotten to put it into words.

Happiness might not be guaranteed in an easy life, but an easy life certainly had fewer heartbreaks. Unfortunately, she hadn't gotten a choice in the cards she'd been dealt.

THE NEXT MORNING they awoke to snow. It was like a mantle had been tossed over Hope while they'd slept, and when Andy crawled out of bed, he'd stared out at drifted peaks. They'd gotten the cattle home just in time.

Andy had asked the drovers to come back this morning to pick up their checks, and there was still another twenty minutes before the drovers were due. The truck bumped and slid over the back drive that led from the fields—he'd just brought some fresh hay for the feeder, the pasture being covered now—and his gaze slid over the peaceful scene. The morning sun was bright and golden, glistening off the fresh snowfall. It covered fields, topped fence posts, and drifted up the sides of buildings—winter's official arrival. The cows congregated in small groups, their breaths coming from their blunt noses in puffs of cloud.

He'd miss this. If he had to be brutally honest, he'd miss Dakota more. He could have been happy enough going back to his life in Billings if it hadn't been for her. She'd awoken him to feelings he wasn't ready for, both for her and for this land he'd thought he'd said goodbye to. But his time with Dakota made him realize exactly what he wanted—everything that was out of reach.

She would come this morning to collect her check and he'd see her again, and his heart sped up at the prospect. He knew where they stood. He knew he couldn't give her the life she deserved, and she knew it all too well. He hoped that this goodbye might make the difference. Maybe if he said goodbye to her in the light of day he'd be able to make his peace with it.

Andy pulled to a stop beside the barn and turned off the engine. His brother had called late last night to say Mackenzie had had the babies and they were doing well. The new arrivals were boys—both over five pounds—and they'd named them Jackson and Jayden. Andy had felt a strange tug of love already for the nephews he was yet to meet—there would be more Granger boys, another set of brothers. He sincerely hoped these two would have a better chance at maintaining a relationship than he and Chet had. The pressures of inheritance and future planning could be disastrous, but these kids would have an uncle who understood all that, and maybe he'd be able to give them some advice about how not to mess things up too badly.

Chet would be coming back to the ranch on his own for a few days before Mackenzie would join him with the babies. That meant Andy's time here would be up and he'd have to bow out and leave the ranch in his brother's capable hands. At the very least, he wanted his brother to come back to everything running as it should. Andy could offer that much.

Andy got out of the vehicle and headed around the side of the barn, snow melting over the leather of his cowboy boots. He stopped short when he saw a figure he recognized—Harley. Andy's hackles immediately rose, remembering Harley's past with cattle rustling. He'd expected Harley to return for his check, but he hadn't expected to see him lurking by the barn door. He appeared to be looking inside rather intently, and he didn't hear Andy as he approached.

Just before Andy spoke, he saw what had Harley's attention. Elliot stood inside the barn, his cell phone to his ear. He was shuffling a boot against the cement floor and leaning against a stall.

"I know. I know…" Elliot was saying. "I was an idiot… I understand why you kicked me out, I do… Yeah, I know. Like I said, I'm sorry about that. I want to be there for our baby and you know what? If you want to get married, I'll do that, too. Your brother said something about a wedding dress your grandmother wore and it got me to thinking…"

"Morning," Andy said quietly, and Harley whirled around.

"Scared me," Harley said with a quiet laugh. "Sorry, I was just—"

Andy raised an eyebrow and Harley shrugged. "He's talking to my sister."

Andy frowned. "He said that she kicked him out." That was news to all of them. They'd been assuming that Elliot and Holly were still together. Had all that drama been for nothing? He had to admit, he liked the idea of this unknown Holly standing up for herself and giving Elliot the boot. If Elliot wasn't going to be man enough to marry her, why should she put up with less?

Except it sounded like Elliot was changing his tune.

"Yeah." Harley scowled down at his boots. "Apparently."

Andy jutted his chin in the direction of the house. "Come with me back to the house. Leave Elliot alone. You don't want to make any more trouble for yourself."

Harley followed Andy away from the door and they headed down the worn path past the chicken coop and toward the house. A frigid wind whipped around the barn and slammed into them as they ducked their heads against the onslaught. Winter was here and they hadn't gotten back a day too soon. If it was this cold here, he was willing to bet the foothills would be freezing.

Harley hunched his shoulders against the cold but his expression was grim.

"You okay?" Andy asked after a moment. "I mean, it's good news, isn't it? Holly didn't take his garbage. She kicked him out. Now you can rest easy. It sounded like he was proposing there, too. She'll have it her way. Mission accomplished, right?"

Harley looked over at Andy then heaved a sigh.

"Why didn't she come home? She'd kicked him

out. She was on her own. There was no reason not
to come back. There was no reason not to open the
door when I knocked."

He felt for the kid. All Harley wanted was to bring
his sister home again where she'd be safe, where he
could protect her, where no one would hurt her. But,
apparently, Holly didn't want that, and Andy could
respect that, too.

"I don't know," Andy said. "Maybe too much
changed."

"Obviously. She's pregnant," Harley retorted.
"Nothing will ever be the same again."

Andy sighed. "Look, kid, I think I get it. Sometimes, when too much changes, when you've changed
too much, there isn't any going home again, only
going forward. Maybe that's why she hasn't come
back—she's not the same girl she used to be and she's
doing the only thing open to her—moving forward."

They stopped at the stairs and kicked the dirt off
their boots before Andy opened the door and they
went inside. The warm air of the kitchen, still scented
with morning coffee and toast, felt good on Andy's
wind-chilled hands. He took off his hat and tossed
it onto the counter, then headed toward the table and
the waiting paychecks.

"I'm her brother." Harley sounded dismal and,
for his sadness, he looked younger still. "I'd be there
for her."

"And you still can be," Andy said. "Maybe she
needs a bit of space."

Sometimes a protective, well-meaning sibling

could be the last thing someone wanted when they were trying to sort out their future. Andy could understand that all too well! He'd had a well-meaning brother of his own, a brother who'd never quite be able to appreciate the depth of his heartache. Holly might be in the same situation right now.

"See…" Andy said after a moment of silence. "We all change. Sometimes home doesn't fit anymore."

Andy picked up the envelopes and flipped through them until he came to Harley's name. He passed it over and Harley accepted it with a nod of thanks.

"I've changed, too," Harley said quietly. "I've been to prison. If that isn't change, I don't know what is. But I still came back again. So I know about home not fitting right anymore, but I also know that if you stick it out, you can find a way to fit in again. It won't be in the same way, but there's always a seat at the table for you. People might need to scoot over a bit, and they might need to fetch another plate, but there's always that seat."

Harley's words slowly sank into Andy's mind and he gave the young man a thoughtful smile. In his mind's eye, he could see those parents waiting for their daughter, still seeing their little girl in spite of it all. Holly could do worse than return to the home that loved her so much. And deep down he wished she'd give in and do just that. At least she had a home to go to. His parents were both gone, and the gap had closed behind him. He should be so lucky.

"You're wise beyond your years, Harley."

"I'm not as young as I look." Harley cast him a lopsided grin.

Andy laughed softly. "Yeah, so you keep saying."

"Thanks for giving me a chance, Mr. Granger," Harley said after a moment. "It was an honor riding with you."

"You bet," Andy said. "Good luck with everything."

"Thank you, sir." Harley turned toward the door, pushing his hat onto his head with one hand.

"Harley," Andy said suddenly, and the young man looked back.

"Yes, sir?"

"What are you going to do about your sister?"

Harley sucked in a deep breath then shrugged. "I don't rightfully know. I'll try and talk to her again, and if she won't talk to me, I'll go home."

"I'm sorry about that," Andy said. "I know it wasn't what you wanted."

Harley smiled. "That's not retreat, that's just doing the next logical thing. Home is home. It isn't going anywhere. We'll be there when she's ready."

"The seat at the table," Andy said quietly.

"You bet, sir. The seat at the table. Thanks again for everything." Harley tapped the brim of his hat then opened the door. A blast of cold air swirled past him into the kitchen and he stepped outside, pulling the door shut behind him.

A seat at the table… Harley seemed pretty optimistic about that, and Andy wondered if there was truth in those words. Was it possible to come home again after letting down your entire community? Was it possible to belong again after years away? There was only one woman he wanted to come home to, and that was Dakota Mason, but Hope had closed up after him. There might be hope for Holly yet, but he doubted there'd be a chance for him.

Unless...

Chapter Thirteen

Dakota stood on a crate, peering under the hood of her truck. The darn thing refused to turn over and she couldn't fetch her paycheck until it did. Her father had the work truck out on the ranch, delivering hay and filling watering troughs, and the other work truck had stopped working last month. She still needed to get the parts to get that one moving, and while she had most of them, she had to make another couple of trips to junkyards to see what she could scavenge. Ordering parts at the auto shop was a last resort.

The sun was higher in the sky but the temperature had most definitely dropped since they'd gotten back from the drive. Her fingers were red with cold. She reached for her travel mug of coffee that sat on the top of the engine block and took a lingering sip of creamy warmth.

Last night they'd gotten several updates from the hospital where Brody was undergoing surgery. All had gone well and they'd been assured that Brody would recover and keep the leg that had been so badly torn apart during the blast. He'd need nursing care when he got back, though, and her parents were already talking about the expense of hiring a full-time nurse.

Dakota had sent her brother several text messages, but she hadn't heard back from him yet. When she finally did, she'd stop worrying, but until then—

An engine rumbled into her drive and she stepped back from the truck and shaded her eyes. It was Andy's vehicle making fresh tracks over the snow-covered driveway, and her heart sped up.

What was he doing here? Didn't he have drovers to pay and a ranch to run? Seeing him again wasn't going to be easy, and she'd counted on being able to steel herself before going over. Having him show up here didn't give her that opportunity.

"Morning!" Andy called as he hopped out of his truck.

"Hi, Andy." She grabbed a rag and wiped at the grease on her hands. "What are you doing here?"

"Bringing your paycheck." He held up an envelope. "You didn't come by to get it, so I thought I'd bring it to you."

"Thanks." She accepted the envelope, trusting that the amount on the check was the amount agreed upon. She'd open it later. When she looked up, she found Andy's eyes locked on her.

"Are you okay?" he asked quietly. "You look… sad."

"It's been a rough night," she admitted. "We got a call that Brody was in an explosion and he's been in surgery. They saved his leg, but—" She swallowed hard. "So he's coming home."

"That's horrible." Andy stepped closer and slid an arm around her waist. She tipped her head against his broad chest, thankful for the brief comfort he provided. "I'm glad he survived, though."

"Me, too," she said. "And I'm glad I didn't end up telling him about Nina or I'd have blamed myself for this."

"Hey, war isn't your fault," he said seriously. "And he's coming home. That's what matters, right?"

She pulled back and nodded quickly. "That's what matters."

"When you open that envelope, you'll find two checks," Andy said. "One is from Chet for your work on the cattle drive and the other is from me."

"What?" She frowned. "Andy, you don't owe me anything—"

"Whatever," he said with a wry smile. "Of course I do. It's my fault you're struggling, and it's the least I can do to get your hydration system."

"I couldn't accept it…" she began. The words evaporated from her mouth as she caught Andy's tender gaze moving over her face and settling at last on her lips. He moved closer and bent his head, catching her lips with his. The softness of his mouth made her forget what she'd been about to say, and she felt like she could melt into his embrace. When he finally pulled back, she asked, "So is that goodbye, then?"

"No, just a kiss."

She felt the color rise in her cheeks. "When do you leave?"

"You're not getting rid of me that easily," he said with a low laugh. "I'm sticking around."

"What?" She could hardly believe her ears. "What are you talking about? I thought you couldn't stay in Hope…that they'd never accept you again, that—"

"I had a weirdly deep talk with Harley," he interrupted her. "As it turns out, Holly had dumped Elliot, after all, but she isn't ready to go home yet. It sounds like Elliot is willing to do pretty much anything to get her back."

"That's really good for them." Dakota smiled. "Harley must be relieved—even if he still isn't Elliot's biggest fan. But how does that change anything for you?"

"He was talking about how no matter how much you change, there is always a place for you at the table, so to speak. It got me to thinking. Anyway, Chet got back this morning. Mack is still in the hospital with the babies, but they should be released in a few days, and Chet asked if I'd stick around. He needs help running the ranch and Mack is going to be pretty busy with the babies, so—"

Dakota realized she'd been holding her breath and she let it out in a sudden rush. "So you're staying?"

Andy nodded. "Good news?"

She felt tears mist her eyes. "Yes…yes! Definitely."

Andy reached out and tucked a stray tendril of hair behind her ear. "I know that your family would never forgive me, but I was wondering if you'd give me a chance to just…be around you. I won't ask for more. Maybe if your family could get to know me, they'd see that I'm a good guy. I'm not the same man I used to be back then, so it won't be the same, but that doesn't mean I can't find home again here in Hope. With you. Just give me the chance to win your father over and then if I can't—"

"Yes." She nodded.

"Yes?" Andy smiled tentatively. "I had a whole speech prepared, you know."

"My dad and I had a talk of our own," she said quietly. "Brody's injury kind of put things into a different perspective for us. Life is short—sometimes too short. We can't waste it on the things that don't matter. He said that he wants me to be happy. He and Brody butted heads for so many years, and he doesn't want to do that to me. So he gave me his blessing to follow my heart. He has no idea that my heart leads to you, but…"

Andy smothered the rest of her words with a kiss and pulled her in close. His strong arms closed around her and she twined her arms up around his neck, leaning into his strength.

"Then marry me," he said, pulling back.

"What?" she gasped.

"I'm serious, marry me! I'm not in this halfway and I'd take my time and wait for you to feel comfortable if I need to do that, but if things have changed and you're willing…" There was pleading in those green eyes. "If you're willing…"

"How would it work?" she asked. "You'd be living with your brother, right?"

"Nope." He grinned. "There are two full ranch houses on that ranch right now—one was our childhood home and the other belonged to Mack's grandmother. I'll be living in the one I grew up in. And, believe me, there's room enough for you, too…and maybe a baby or two of our own."

"Is this really possible?" she asked in disbelief.

"Which part?" he teased. "The baby or the wedding? Because I happen to know a minister who could marry us tomorrow if you wanted to get started on the babies…"

"Andy!" She blushed and shook her head.

Andy lifted her hand to his lips, looked at it for a moment, turned it over and then kissed the one clean spot on the back of her wrist.

"I'm in love with you, Dakota. I want to marry you. I'm completely serious, and I'll prove that I was the better choice for the rest of your life, if you'll let me."

"I love you, too," she whispered. "And, yes, I'll marry you."

Andy moved in for another kiss and she planted a hand on his chest, holding him back. "But one more thing," she said.

"Anything." She could see by the look in his eye that he meant it. The tenderness in his face promised so much more than words ever could.

"When we tell my dad about this," she said quietly, "you're going to have to duck. His first reaction isn't going to be pleasant."

Andy chuckled softly and pulled her back into his arms, his lips hovering over hers. "That's a deal. Hope couldn't be home without you in it." He paused, holding back just a whisper away from a kiss. "I'm a lucky guy."

Joy bubbled up inside her and Dakota grinned into Andy's warm, green eyes. "You most certainly are. Now kiss me already."

And Andy did. He kissed her long and slow, and when he finally released her, Dakota was certain that while they'd have a whole knot to untie when it came to her family, Andy Granger was most certainly worth all the trouble he was going to cause. This love would be the foundation for their very own home. And Hope, Montana, was just big enough for them all.

Epilogue

The Christmas Eve wedding was Chet's idea.

"Mom would have liked that," he said. "Besides, you need something to celebrate again, Andy. It's different for me now that I have Mack and the boys. It changes your focus, gives you someone to put a Christmas together *for*. But I'd say start now—make your Christmases your anniversary, too. Love is what Christmas is all about, isn't it?"

"Who would even come?" Andy asked. "I'm Enemy Number One around here."

"The ones who love you," Chet said. "Make it an intimate wedding. Let everyone else wonder how it went down."

It had made a lot of sense and when Andy asked Dakota what she'd thought, she'd immediately agreed. Planning a wedding in three weeks flat was a whirlwind affair, and it took both families pulling together to make it happen.

Unfortunately, Brody wasn't back in time for the wedding, which was disappointing for everyone. He got an infection in his leg and had to stay another few weeks in the VA hospital, but they set up a webcam so he could watch the entire thing from his hospital bed.

On the morning of Christmas Eve, when Andy stood in a sunlit church with his bride, the minister's words tumbling around them, he could feel all those childhood Christmases coming back again... the love, the anticipation, the bone-deep certainty that with Dakota he'd finally come home.

The actual ceremony was a blur. He'd promised himself he'd remember every second of it, but all he'd remember later was looking down in those chocolate-brown eyes of her and saying "I do" with every fiber of his being. She wore a long ivory dress with lace sleeves, her soft skin peeking through. A long veil fell back from her dark hair, cascading down over her shoulders into a frothy pool around her feet. She was promising to be his, to be Mrs. Dakota Granger until death parted them.

But it was the memories made later at the reception, in an antiques neighbor's barn renovated for social events, that would settle into Andy's heart. As they stepped into the candlelit room for the first time as husband and wife, Dakota tugged him to a stop and he looked up to find a spray of mistletoe hanging above them.

"Merry Christmas, Andy," Dakota whispered, her eyes glistening in the low light.

He dipped his head and kissed her gently, tugging her close to him, wishing they had fewer observers for this...

Every table around the room had a sprig of mistletoe, and Andy felt his throat close off with emotion as he looked around at the glossy barn filled with the people who supported them—more than he'd imagined would be there. Chet was persuasive, and after Ken Mason's initial reaction of rage, after Dakota'd had a long talk with her dad out in a field—a talk that took an entire morning—Ken turned out to be pretty persuasive, too.

There was room at the family table—it just took a little shifting of the chairs.

And every Christmas thereafter, in Andy and Dakota's home, after the kids were born and as the years crept by, Dakota would put up mistletoe around the house, surprising Andy with a kiss when he happened underneath it. It was a tradition started by Andy's mom when she'd thought she was being playful but really was etching her love into her family's hearts. Andy's kids would grow up with the same laughter and outpouring of love, and mistletoe began to mean something a little more in Hope, Montana.

It was more than "Merry Christmas." It was the meaning of Christmas…love, family and the sound of the angels in a woman's loving voice saying, "Look up—mistletoe!"

* * * * *

Brody Mason returns from Afghanistan badly injured, but his physical wounds don't compare to the emotional pain of learning his fiancée married his best friend. Only one woman can heal this troubled cowboy...and she'll never settle for being his second choice.

Watch for THE COWBOY'S VALENTINE BRIDE (February 2017), the next book in Patricia Johns's compelling HOPE, MONTANA miniseries.

Available December 6, 2016

#1621 THE COWBOY SEAL'S JINGLE BELL BABY

Cowboy SEALs • by Laura Marie Altom

Fresh off a mission, Navy SEAL Rowdy Jones comes home to a six-month-old voice mail from Tiffany Lawson. Not only is she pregnant, but she's planning on giving his baby up for adoption!

#1622 THE RANCHER AND THE BABY

Forever, Texas • by Marie Ferrarella

Will Laredo and his best friend's sister, Cassidy McCullough, put their differences aside to rescue an orphaned baby. Now they must care for their new charge—and maybe realize they're made for each other in the process.

#1623 A MONTANA CHRISTMAS REUNION

Snowy Owl Ranchers • by Roz Denny Fox

Jewell Hyatt broke Saxon Conrad's heart years ago because she couldn't see a future together. After a one-night reunion, Jewell discovers she's pregnant. Is a future with Saxon possible the second time around?

#1624 TWINS FOR CHRISTMAS

Welcome to Ramblewood • by Amanda Renee

Barrel racer Hannah Tanner is raising her best friend's orphaned two-year-old daughters. Until their biological father appears, ready to claim them. He'll never get her girls, but can she stop him from stealing her heart?

HWESTCNM1116

REQUEST YOUR FREE BOOKS!
2 FREE NOVELS PLUS 2 FREE GIFTS!

HARLEQUIN®

Western Romance

ROMANCE THE ALL-AMERICAN WAY!

HWR16

SPECIAL EXCERPT FROM

⊕ **HARLEQUIN**®
™

༄Western ᴫomance

*Will Laredo and Cassidy McCullough have been at odds
since they were kids, until they rescue a baby and find
themselves fighting attraction instead of each other.*

Read on for a sneak preview of
THE RANCHER AND THE BABY,
the next book in USA TODAY *bestselling author*
Marie Ferrarella's **FOREVER, TEXAS** *miniseries.*

She raised her eyes again, expecting to meet his, but Will
was once again strictly focused on the road ahead. She felt
something almost weird for a second.

"Are we having a moment here?" she asked him.

Will wasn't able to read her tone of voice and decided
that the wisest thing was just to acknowledge her words in
the most general possible sense.

"I suppose that some people might see it that way," he
said.

Cassidy shook her head. "Typical."

"Come again?"

Cassidy raised her voice. "I said your answer's typical.
You're a man who has never committed to anything."

"Not true." Will contradicted her before he could think
better of it.

"Okay, name one thing," she challenged.

She was not going to box him in if that was what
she was looking to do, he thought. At least, not about
something that was way too personal to talk about out
loud with her. Besides, he did just fine having everyone

think that he was only serious about any relationship he had for a very limited amount of time. That way, if he brought about the end himself, he never had to publicly entertain the sting of failure.

"I'm committed to restoring my father's ranch, making it into the paying enterprise it should have been and still could be with enough effort," he told her.

"You mean that?"

Rather than say yes, he told her, "I never say something just to hear myself talk."

"There's some difference of opinion on that one, but—"

"Look," he began, about to tell her that he didn't want to get into yet another dispute with her over what amounted to nothing, but he never had the opportunity. The one thing that Cassidy admittedly could do better than anyone he knew was outtalk everyone.

"—if you're really serious about that," she was saying, "I can probably manage to help you out a few hours on the weekends." The way she saw it, she did owe it to him for helping her save the baby, and she hated owing anyone, most of all him.

Will spared her a glance before he went back to watching the road intently. Cassidy had managed to do the impossible.

She had rendered him completely speechless.

Don't miss
THE RANCHER AND THE BABY
by Marie Ferrarella, available December 2016
wherever Harlequin® Western Romance®
books and ebooks are sold.

www.Harlequin.com

HWREXP1116

HARLEQUIN®

A *Romance* FOR EVERY MOOD™

Stay up-to-date on all your
romance-reading news with the
Harlequin Shopping Guide,
featuring bestselling authors, exciting new
miniseries, books to watch and more!

The newest issue will be delivered right to you
with our compliments! There are 4 each year.

Signing up is easy.

EMAIL

ShoppingGuide@Harlequin.ca

WRITE TO US

HARLEQUIN BOOKS
Attention: Customer Service Department
P.O. Box 9057, Buffalo, NY 14269-9057

OR PHONE

1-800-873-8635 in the United States
1-888-343-9777 in Canada

Please allow 4-6 weeks for delivery of the first issue by mail.